The Erotic Adventures

of Johnny Johnson

The Erotic Adventures

of

Johnny Johnson

An Autobiography* by Johnny Johnson

*(Completely true and absolutely factual in every aspect)

Vincto Publishing

Copyright

Vincto Publishing

Acknowledgements

This book would never have happened without the support, feedback and crazy brainstorming of some very special people.

My deepest and longest thanks to Claire Fletcher, Michael Seigal and Matthew Webb—and all those others who've been with me on this journey.

Snickles font used under Creative Commons attribution license with thanks to Tup Wanders http://www.tupwanders.nl
Pacifico font copyright (c) 2011, Vernon Adams (vern@newtypography.co.uk), with Reserved Font Name Pacifico. This Font Software is licensed under the SIL Open Font License, Version 1.1. http://scripts.sil.org/OFL
Lips artwork adapted from original photo "Estudio sobre una boca "by Carlos Adampol Galindo shared under Creative Commons Attribution-Share Alike 2.0 Generic license. https://www.flickr.com/people/11767501@N07
Vector artwork courtesy of PublicDomainVectors.org

Contents

Foreword

This book is crude, crass and perverted.

I'm begging you; do not under any circumstances read this book.

Unless, of course, you are crude, crass and perverted yourself, in which case you might find it funny.

Names have been changed to protect the innocent. Oh, and the adulterers too.

Chapter 1: Micropenis

"What d'you say, doc; am I the luckiest guy in the world?"

I laid back on the inspection table and the doctor, a very sleek and sexy woman of, I would guess of Chinese or Japanese descent, was examining my crotch with one of those magnifying glass things that had a bright light attached. She wore a black turtleneck and a white coat, and her name tag said Dr. Yu. Where in Asia does a name like Yu come from? As my thoughts drifted I realized the smell of antiseptic combined with the professionalism of a serious medical examination was deeply reassuring.

She reached for my chart, and after scanning it for a few seconds she slid her glasses down her nose and looked at me, with what I later would discover to have been pity in her eyes.

"Not exactly, Mr. Johnson."

"Call me Johnny, doc."

My name had been a cruel irony throughout my teenage years and beyond. I guess people automatically assume that a guy called Johnson—and Johnny Johnson at that—would have a fairly hefty meat mallet. From the first girl I sweet talked into the backseat of my car, to every subsequent date I thought I was getting lucky on, the show stopped when my shorts dropped and they got their look at my micropenis.

Every disastrous date led to the situation I found myself in this morning, waking on my twenty-fourth birthday; a virgin. But this morning was unlike any that had gone before, for as I reached down to reassure my morning glory I grasped a surprisingly hefty appendage. I threw back the sheets, my heartbeat racing and there, gloriously erect, was a penis that would make a bull jealous.

The next blissful hour I spent photographing it, washing it and singing happy birthday songs around my apartment, but as the first flush of elation faded into a happy glow, I felt a moment of unease. Realizing that it was quite a sudden change to overcome a guy, I thought I'd better seek a professional opinion.

"I'm afraid I have some bad news for you, Mr. Johnson."

"Please doc, just call me Johnny. So, what's your professional opinion?"

She took off her glasses, closed her eyes and pinched the brow of her nose.

"Johnny... there is no easy way to tell you this, so I'll just come out and say it. You have cancer of the penis. You have—at best—twenty-four hours to live, and the only way we can save your life is to amputate your penis before you die."

Needless to say, I was stunned.

"Doc... are you sure?"

Then came denial.

"I don't believe you! How could God grant me this magnificent cock and then only give me a day to live?"

Then a ray of hope. The sexy doctor laid her hand on my bare thigh, slowly sliding it higher up my leg.

"Johnny, please calm down. I've counseled many terminally ill people and the one lesson we take from this is that each day could be your last; whether you are healthy or sick. You need to live everyday with everything you have. Go out there Johnny, have the best day of your life, but for God's sake get back here within twenty-four hours so that I can operate and save your life."

This story is about the last day of my life.

"Doc..."

She raised her hand, lingering with a fingertip before walking away, long slim legs in dark tights disappearing up inside her white coat. She stopped at a glass cabinet full of specimen jars. Large urns with ghostly organs floating in pale yellow suspension.

"Call me Felicia, Felicia Yu, Mr. Johnson or... Johnny, if I may. The thing is, I have a confession to make. I have a peccadillo, a fetish if you will, for medical abnormalities. To be frank, that was the reason I studied medicine. The irregularities of the human body... well Johnny; the truth is that they make me hot."

She turned to face me but her gaze was fixed on my tumescence.

Felicia took off her glasses and tied back her long straight black hair.

"Johnny, I think I can improve your mood, if not your prognosis..." After taking a long drink from her mug of coffee she walked around the examination table and positioned herself between my feet, then grasped my ankles and pulled me toward her.

The random panic that had been screaming in my mind cleared like a cold shower as she moistened her rosebud lips. She looked up at my face, for once, and smiled, then she leaned forward and I felt her hot breath on my pulsing tip.

Chapter 2: Flashback

Right about now you'll be wondering how my mind could possibly be wandering, but some things can only be properly explained through the judicious use of a flashback. So cue a dissolving picture and some wavy lines.

Twenty-four Years Ago

Saint Tristram of the Improbable Annunciation Memorial Hospital

Picture, if you will, a surgically white room and a red-faced, panting woman with shiny, sweaty skin, lying on a surgically white bed. A nurse and a doctor standing between her splayed feet and a bawling, placenta-splattered infant being wiped clean.

"Well done, Mrs. Johnson, very well done. It's all over now." The doctor peered at the new-born baby, adjusted his horn-rimmed glasses and frowned.

The father, holding his wife's white-knuckled grip with his left hand, pumped the air vigorously with his right fist.

"Alright! Woo-hoo! A boy—and what a boy!"

The doctor straightened up and shook his head slowly. "That's the umbilical cord, Mr. Johnson. It comes off."

"Aww..." Mr. Johnson's pumping fist dropped, and he patted for the cigar in his breast pocket.

The doctor cleared his throat. "Your son, whilst in every other way appearing to be a fine healthy chap, does have an uncommon but unfortunate condition. I'm afraid to say, he has been born with a micropenis."

My mother later told me that she had seen my father only cry once before, when he was told that Elvis had died, but on the day I was born his hysterical shrieking was so extreme that he had to be sedated.

Time to do some more wavy lines, and if you like, the faint sound of water going down a drain. Another flashback.

Ten Years Ago
Smalltown High School

I'd say my younger years were quite normal. I played with the neighborhood kids, Gwen Hertzensbrecher from next door and Marcus Goldenrod from across the street. We had tree-houses, patrolled the streets on our bikes, and discovered (and adopted) interesting insects. We shrieked as we bombed the pool in the summer, laughed as we slid down snowy hillsides in the winter, dressed up for Halloween, and groaned as we were sick behind the same bushes. Things only started to go downhill when I arrived at high school, which I guess was when I first started realizing how I felt about Gwen.

Seared onto my fragile adolescent memory is that terrible day when everything just fell apart. Dad had just pulled away from the school in his big blue Ford, and I was standing there, looking up at the new high school with my best pal, Marcus, standing beside me.

Gwen was up by the school entrance, standing with a group of girls, and they were all giggling together. Teenage hormones made me uncomfortable and nervous, then Gwen looked over to me and pointed. They all started to shriek with laughter.

"Marcus? Why is Gwen laughing at me? Why are they all laughing at me?"

The white leather sleeve of a varsity jacket fell across my shoulder and with it a firm hug from Marcus.

"Buddy. I'm so sorry, but Gwen told everyone you had a micropenis and now the rest of your life will be hell. Tough break, champ."

I slumped to my knees, tears starting to well up in my eyes, and with a slow shake of his head Marcus walked away and left me to my misery.

I won't take you through each bitter blow, but I'm sure you get the picture now. Teased and tormented. The weekly locker room and shower time indignation. The stony wall of silence any time I tried to talk to a girl. Gwen ignored me from that day on as well, but what made it hurt the most was that I knew I still loved her. And I hated myself for it. Why couldn't I just hate her like any normal guy? Well, I didn't have a chance for a rebound, or any bound of any kind. I had a micropenis and that became the measure of my social life.

And Marcus? Well we just grew apart, these things happen when you get older. Straight out of high school, skipping college altogether, he founded «Awesome Computers» where he completely revolutionized the whole computer industry by making the incredibly bold and innovative decision to sell computers in white cases unlike everyone else who stuck to black.

Oh, and I also heard that he started dating Gwen Hertzensbrecher too. Entrepreneur billionaire and dating the most beautiful girl in the world. When you see what an awesome guy like him who has everything can achieve, then you understand what a worthless loser I am.

Right up to yesterday I lived up to my role perfectly.

Growing up as a sexually frustrated young virgin is a daily cycle between sleep, wank, food, wank and surfing the internet. Mostly in preparation for more wanking. I had become a master of masturbation. I probably deserved a black belt. Because of my rigorous training, and the manner in which I engage in the aforementioned activity, my thumb and forefinger are so well exercised I can bend pennies with one hand.

That was the life I found myself in, waking up in my loser apartment that I could only barely afford the rent for. My extremely limited wage from the job I'd sought out in a tabletop gaming shop where I could be guaranteed to be spared the embarrassment of ever having to talk to a female. Did I not like women? My two tube a week KY-Jelly habit was testament to the contrary, but I was just tired of the rejection and humiliation. I had one, (1), uno female connection on FriendBook, and that was my mother. My most frequent engagement with the fairer sex was by proxy of a two-dimensional representation.

Now all that pent up sexual energy coursed through my body as Dr. Felicia Yu's lips parted an inch above the purple pulsing tip of my massive new erection.

"Johnny... I don't think I can fit it all into my mouth... but I'm damn well going to try."

And she really did.

Chapter 3: The Gucci, the Porsche and the Redhead

Ah my first blow job. Bliss. I wanted it to last longer, wanted to be able to hold back but as soon as she wrapped her hands around the base of my shaft and started tugging in time with the bobbing of her head, I was doomed. I came like The Force and unloaded into Dr. Yu's throat. I lay there panting and spent, wallowing in a glut of pleasure and post-orgasm hormones. She took a couple of sips of her cold coffee, then wiped me clean with some surgical wipes, the mild alcohol cooling as it evaporated, tingling and turning my mind to further exploits.

"That was amazing, Felicia. How would you like to try something else out, you know, for medical research?"

Her glasses went back on and suddenly she was a cool professional again. "I'm afraid your appointment is over, Mr. Johnson. I have another patient waiting."

I groaned, feeling my rigidity very much unresolved. "Am I still technically a virgin?"

She tapped her lips with a pencil as she considered my case. "Technically yes, but I don't have time to help you with that right now. I need you out of my office so you'll have to find someone else to take things further."

I got dressed and, thanking the ghost of Levi Strauss for loose-fitting jeans, was able to button myself in. The bulge was quite noticeable and a felt a giddy wave of elation looking down on it. On impulse I gave Felicia a quick hug and a peck on the cheek which she bore with calm dignity.

"Thanks doc. I really mean it."

"Don't thank me yet Mr. Johnson. Remember, twenty-four hours and not a minute longer."

I looked at my watch. A quarter past nine. "Got it. Back here tomorrow. See ya then, doc."

"Oh, and Mr. Johnson?"

"Mmm?"

"Although sexual activity is probably good for you and will help reduce the pressure in your penis, you might want to gloss over the fact that your massive erection is actually a tumor if you meet any other women. I think my personal preferences are likely to be unique—"

"Got it. Regular old huge cock. I'll remember that."

Then she shooed me out the door.

I took the bus back downtown and immediately cursed the moment I stepped off outside my apartment block.

"Johnny! Cooee!"

I shuddered. Mrs. Robertson waved at me from the steps leading up to our communal front door. Mrs. Robertson was the wrong side of fifty, plump, and gushed generously over the tight purple dress she was wearing. Her bouffant blonde hairdo and hooker-red lipstick, combined with a cleavage you could park a bike in would make her a very welcome sight... if you were viewing her through very thick beer goggles.

I however was stone-cold sober and swallowed weakly as I approached.

"Hey, Mrs. Robertson..."

"Linda, Johnny, please call me Linda; in fact," she fluttered her eyelashes like two sexually aggressive spiders bobbing on their webs. "Just call me."

I edged past her, my back to the wall, but she stepped in close, pressing her pillowy breasts against my chest and resting her hand on my shoulder. Horrified onlooker syndrome took hold and my gaze was irresistibly drawn down the mammary mountains spilling over the top of her low cut dress.

"Johnny..." her breathless lips were less than an inch from mine. "It must be so lonely for you in that apartment alone all the time. I'm lonely too... we should be more companionable—oh!"

Her hand strayed down my chest, around my hips and finally to my swollen groin.

This close you could see how much makeup she had slathered on to cover her wrinkles. Mrs. Robertson did that thing with her eyelashes again and gave me a squeeze.

"We can't let this go to waste, can we Johnny?"

I squeaked as fumbled with my keys, poking them ineffectually at the lock like an incompetent Casanova until they finally turned. I squeezed my way past her and through the door.

"Johnny!"

"Sorry Mrs. Robertson, I really need to go... I'm late, maybe—" I bit my lip and bolted for the stairs, taking them two at a time.

"Oh Johnny..."

My door slammed shut and I bolted and chained it. I leaned back against the door, listening for the stairs, but I was safe. I sighed and slid down to the floor. Mrs. Robertson was usually more persistent. Lucky for me she was sober this morning, for once.

My heart rate slowed and I picked myself up. I checked my watch. 9:44, no time to waste on the last day of my life. I flung open my wardrobe and looked at my carefully folded jeans and T-shirts featuring colorful superheroes, ironed and hung on coat hangers. Not exactly chick magnet apparel. I knew something had to be done.

There was one last thing I needed. By my bed I had a chest of drawers and underneath some old photos and a watch I hadn't worn for years was a carefully folded piece of paper. I pulled it out and spread it open. This was The List.

If Hollywood ever makes a movie about my life, they are bound to call it *The List*. They like succinct titles like that. At my college graduation the dean brought in a motivational speaker. Someone to send us off with fire in our bellies and the burning need to change the world. He was okay, mostly just plugging his NYT Best Seller, but halfway through he said something that really resonated with me on that day. He said to make a list of all the things you wanted to do before you die, cross them off when you achieve them or add new ones as they come along. As I celebrated, alone in my room, slowly getting drunker and drunker, I made a list. I never threw it away, but I never crossed anything off it either. You'll understand why when I read you a few examples.

Number 3: Bang a hot brunette
Number 19: Nail a hot Russian chick

And so on. You get the general idea. I've pulled out The List every now and then, usually by accident, but each time if solidly failed to motivate me in any way. It taunted me, and I'm not too proud to say that on occasions it brought me to tears. Today however, it brought a broad smile to my face. I picked up a well-chewed biro and drew a line through one, and then with a shrug through another.

Number 2: Get a blow job
Number 8: Score with a hot Asian babe

Motivated now? Hell yes.

I folded The List, stashed it in my wallet, and changed into a plain white T-shirt. After checking out the window in case Mrs. Robertson was loitering with intent, I headed uptown. I was a warm morning and despite my impending doom I felt a glow of potential rise in my heart as I began to accept my true challenge to live this day like my last. Also, my cock was throbbing so hard I felt if I didn't get release soon then I would faint.

The first ATM I saw found me with drawing all my life's savings, which amounted to nothing more than a couple of thousand bucks. I crossed to a bank and signed up for a credit card, then another, then another. Buy now and nothing to pay for thirty days? Ha! Suckers.

The pharmacy was next. Right beside the pregnancy test kits were row after row of different condoms. Extra thin, extra thick, colored, flavored, ridged or knobbled. I flushed and felt a momentary dizziness. I had never paid much attention to this stuff before and was feeling out of my depth. Ah hell. There are sizes too. I really should have measured the cheeky fellow before I left my place.

I approached the counter and laid two packets on the counter. A bespectacled middle-aged woman looked up at me with only a faint effort of feigning interest.

"Is there anything else, or will that be all—"

"I wanted to ask..." my cheeks started burning up. I knew I shouldn't be embarrassed for buying condoms at twenty-four but it was my first time, damn it and I felt like a kid again. "Which of these is, erm, the, you know, largest?"

She turned each pack over and adjusted her glasses. "Well," she said squinting at the fine print, "says here that the XXL is a bit longer, but the Extreme Max is for more girth."

I just wanted to get the hell out of here when she said the word 'girth'. "I'll take them both, thanks."

She sighed and ran them through the register. "Shall I bag them for you?"

"No, I'm fine." I tore open the cartons and emptied them into my pockets, left the boxes on the counter and made a hasty retreat.

"Geek," I heard her mutter. "Probably just making water balloons or something."

Breathing deeply I made it to the street. This was a good part of town and there was a classy men's outfitter's across from the pharmacy with dapper Italian suit-clad dummies in the windows.

Carlyles' Sartorial Emporium

I stepped inside and immediately received a smirk from the elderly man in a pinstripe suit who greeted me.

"Can I help you?" He surveyed my scruffy Levis and his nostril twitched.

"Yes, I—"

"Maybe sir is lost? The Gap is just a few minutes down the road."

I had too much to do today to stand around and get taunted by shop assistants.

"Listen Cyril Sneer, I don't care what you think about my dress sense, because I'm leaving here with something smooth and sexy."

I slapped down my new credit cards on the glass topped counter and pointed at a mannequin with a slim-cut dark navy suit. He looked about my size.

"That looks pretty good. I'll try it on."

"Sir. That is a three-thousand dollar Gucci."

I shrugged. "If chicks dig it then so do I."

With a labored sigh he removed the jacket from the mannequin and held it open so I could slip my arms inside. I fastened the top button, smoothed it down and examined myself in the mirror. I looked damn sharp.

"Nice. I'll take it."

Cyril brushed an invisible piece of fluff from my shoulders and sniffed. "It does make sir look a tad more refined. Should I measure for trouser adjustments?"

"Knock yourself out Cyril."

He knelt in front of me with one end of a measuring tape at my ankle, then began to draw the other end up my inner leg.

"Does sir dress to the left or right—Good God!"

My victory complete, I shared a grin with my equally triumphant reflection. "Yes Cyril; that's all me. Just make it a bit baggy around the knees. I like a bit of airflow."

Cyril stood up visibly paler than when I'd first walked in. He coughed and shuffled behind the cash register and hit some buttons.

"That will be three thousand dollars, sir. The pants will be ready in a few hours."

I slid the nearest card across the counter to him and pocketed the others.

Stepping out onto the sidewalk I took a deep breath and knew that the saying was true, a good suit would make a man out of you. And with that thought in my mind I spied *Elite Prestige Rentals* across the street. There were low-slung red sports cars and glistening silver limousines parked out front. May as well blow everything, I reasoned; I wouldn't be needing it tomorrow.

A bell pinged as I pushed the door open and it rattled as it shut behind me. A skinny redhead with coppery curls that fell to her shoulders looked up from her magazine and smiled at me.

"Good morning sir. How may I help you?"

I smiled back, trying to appear suave and manly, and not at all creepy. My palms were getting damp. I cleared my throat and glanced at her name badge, which read '*Hi, my name is Kirsten*'. It was pinned on the lapel of a white blouse that was so tight it looked like it had been sprayed on. Every contour of her black brassiere that cupped her pert boobies was visible through the translucent fabric; she didn't have a lot but she was showing it all off. And just a hint maybe of nipple visible? Oh God I'm just standing here staring at her tits!

"Hi Kirsten, sorry, I was having a bit of difficulty reading that badge. I, uh, I have a touch of astigmatism..."

"Oh I'm sorry, you mean your joints ache in cold weather?"

"Wait what? No! No that is rheumatism. Astigmatism is bad eyesight."

"Oh right, I get it. Bad eyesight. I just thought you were staring at my tits."

"No, really, I was trying to make out your name badge. I just came in here to rent a car."

"We have prestige cars only, sir. Are we within your, ah, budget?" She nodded to my scuffed sneakers.

I straightened the lapels of my three-thousand dollar suit that was, so far, not living up to my expectations. "Now listen here, miss. I came here to rent the fastest sports car you have. If you don't want my business then I'll take it elsewhere—"

"No, sir wait! I apologize. The economy has been hard on everyone. Even people with money aren't flashing it around as much as they used to. It's been hard on businesses like ours. Please, let me show you what we have in the yard out back, if you don't see what you like I can make a few calls. I definitely won't let you leave here unsatisfied."

I grinned. "So you're 100% commission paid then?"

It was an ice-breaker, she laughed. "Yeah, pretty much. Here, come with me."

She lead me through a corridor lined with framed photos of classic sports cars, and out to a large parking lot. There were a couple of rows of well-polished cars. Kirsten stopped by the first, a dark grey BMW.

"You get good mileage from this one." She slid her hand down the car's flank and I had an involuntary quiver remembering Felicia's hand on my leg an hour earlier.

Kirsten quirked an eyebrow at me, swaying on the spot. "Sir? Are you okay?"

I pulled myself together and coughed into my fist. "Yes fine, my mind was just wandering. Where were we?"

"The BMW?"

"Oh right. I mean no. Meh. It just that its—"

"Tame. I totally understand, sir. You want something that stands out. Makes an impression?"

"Yes, exactly. What else do you have?"

She sauntered down the row of cars. How she was able to walk at all that black pencil skirt was beyond me, yet she managed it with grace, her pert buttocks rising and falling with each step. She turned around and I managed to raise my head just in time. She smiled as she slid her backside along the edge of a banana-yellow torpedo with wheels.

"How about a classic Ferrari? Girls love them."

"Really? Are you saying I should take this one?"

"Why not? Don't you like it?"

"Well, yeah, of course. But..." What did she mean that girls love Ferraris? Was I missing something?

She crossed her arms over those pert little boobies. "You don't look convinced. Tell me. What is it you are really looking for?"

Wait, was she hitting on me now? Oh God I'm so confused. "It's just that I wanted something... well I had my heart set on something red, you know?"

The flash of her white smile made my heart skip a beat. Damn. What was a girl this sexy doing in a car rental store? She should be modeling or be in movies. She grabbed me by the wrist and dragged me to the end of the line of cars.

"There. That's the one for you, isn't it?"

Curved, squat, lean, elegant. Candy red Porsche. Convertible of course. This was the one.

She opened the door and ushered me into the driver's seat and I sunk into the leather cocoon, breathing in that new car smell and squeezing the steering wheel.

"It's a thousand dollars a day, with a five thousand dollar excess to be held on your credit card."

I shrugged. "Whatever." The money was valueless to me, and there would be no creditors where I'd be tomorrow.

"Wow. You really are loaded. What line of work are you in?"

"Umm...ah internet entrepreneur. Yeah, that's it. Oh and international gigolo, heh. That's what this car makes me feel like."

She smiled at me. "Keep your secrets then. I was just curious to see what a cute guy your age would do for a job to be able to throw around so much cash."

She thinks I'm cute? Is that what it takes to make a pretty girl like you; a fast car and an expensive suit? Guess so.

"Well, I..."

"Let me show you all the switches. Ignition here, wipers here, indicators here."

She leaned across me pointing at the stereo and still saying something that I wasn't really concentrating on and her hair brushed my face. The side of her body was against my chest and I smelt her perfume and felt her warmth. She wriggled forward an inch, pulling open the glove box and pressing her breast into my shoulder. I felt my breathing quicken and grow shallow.

"Sir? A little help?"

"Sorry, what? I was miles away."

"I said would you mind helping me get back out? I think I'm stuck and I don't want to rip my new skirt."

I cleared my throat. "Yes, yes of course." Both my arms were trapped under her body and against my lap. I tried to lift her but the steering wheel got in the way, so I tried to roll her toward me.

"That's my breast," she mentioned.

"I..." My throat was constricted and my cock started to throb. She wriggled back a bit and I watched those two perfect buns in her pencil skirt flex and stretch the taut fabric.

"Wow. You must work out a lot. Your thigh is like iron!" She gripped me and gave me a quick squeeze.

"That's... that's not my thigh." I felt the pressure mounting and thought that if I didn't get some release I would explode.

"Oh... OH!" She slid back enough, dragging her body along my trouser tent, until she got her toes on the ground and struggled to her feet. "You're still holding my breast."

My hand still cupped her budding tit and one of her blouse buttons had popped open during her transit of my lap. The lacy bridge in the middle of her bra was visible, above and below it pale creamy flesh.

"And you're still holding my..." Her fingers were wrapped firmly around my trapped penis. It pulsed for each heartbeat and for each pulse she gave it a squeeze.

"Cock," she said, and grinned at me. "Tell me the truth. When you walked in, were you looking at my name tag or my tits?"

My mouth was dry and my tongue felt like an insole. "Tits," I said weakly.

"Are you going to take a better look?" She ran the heel of her hand slowly up and down my erection, fingertips rotating around my tip where my jeans had a damp spot.

"Okay..." I reluctantly released her soft mound and with trembling fingers undid her collar button. My thumbs parted the cloth and brushed against the skin of her throat. Warm satin.

She flushed down her neck, a rosy hue against the strands of her red hair. "Keep going," she said as she placed her knee between my legs, her pencil skirt rode up to her hips, and she settled herself astride my trouser trapped tool. I gasped as I felt the heat of her sex through my jeans and fumbled with the next button on her blouse.

"Ooo." Her eyelids fluttered closed as she rubbed herself against me and I tore through the remaining buttons, spreading her blouse at the shoulders then cautiously running my fingers across her skin and over the black lace.

She hitched her skirt up higher and I glanced down to see her tiny black lace panties. A thong ran over each hip, securing a two-inch triangle. She slipped a finger under the lace and rubbed the base of my cock through it and my jeans.

"I'm Kirsten, what's your name?"

I had to open my mouth twice before words came out. "Johnny..."

"Fuck me Johnny. Fuck me in this car."

She started working on my belt, then my buttons, all the while grinding against me.

"Why are you trembling, Johnny? I would have thought you had girls just throwing themselves at you all the time?"

My head lolled back against the leather head rest as I struggled to breathe, then in a glorious moment of clarity I knew that this is everything I'd dreamed of, all those years of longing and frustration. Finally I was going to lose my virginity, and with a spectacularly gorgeous woman who was completely in lust with me.

I tugged down the lace of her bra to a gasp from Kristen at each moment, running fingertips across the narrow puckered ring of her pink areola as they emerged. Teasing her and teasing myself before pulling the cloth completely down and exposing her rigid little nipples. She gasped as gently took hold of them and rolled them between my fingers, then she leaned forward, pressing her little mounds against my face, dragging them back and forth against my lips until I suckled each one to the symphony of her sighs.

"I need you," she said, her fingers running through my hair and clasping my head against her.

Her moaning and grinding were driving me to the point of release. I released reluctantly my nibbling lips and glanced around the parking lot. It was as still and quiet as when we'd entered so I began to wriggle my pants down and free my cock. She squealed with each thrust as I bumped her off my lap, then landing on me again until I had my jeans down to my knees and my cock was released.

"Johnny... it's massive!" She raised herself up and pulled the tiny thong to the side revealing the palest pink lips below a triangle of russet fluff. She brushed my tip up and down and her sex kissed me.

She smiled at me as I groaned, feeling sure I couldn't last much longer. I fumbled in my pocket and brought out a foil-wrapped packet.

"Good boy. Well prepared." She rolled the raincoat down my shaft then resumed brushing my tip against her.

"Please..." My hands gripped her narrow hips, urging her onto me.

"Yes," she said and she sank slowly down my length as I groaned deeply, ecstatically and her heat enveloped me. "Oh Johnny." She ground against me, wrapping her arms around my neck, returning her nipple to my lips and moaning in my ear. I slid my hands under her blouse and around her waist, then up the softness of her back to the catch of her brassiere. I groped around and got perhaps one hook undone before giving up. Her skirt was around her waist so I grabbed her butt cheeks and squeezed in time with my thrusting.

"Harder Johnny. Harder!"

Not needing a second invitation I began to buck my hips harder. Suddenly the horn blared and a spasm of shock ran through me. My head whiplashed to each side thinking someone had caught us before realizing it was Kirsten's lovely bottom bouncing off the steering wheel.

She slapped me, then grabbed me by my hair. "Don't stop, I'm nearly there!" Her other hand was between her legs and as I started bucking up into her, horn blaring with every stroke, she moaned and her eyelids fluttered at half-mast and she started to convulse. Her contractions pushed me over the edge and I joined her in that ecstasy.

She sighed and slumped against me, nuzzling into my neck and whispering so softly I couldn't make out the words. My arms went around her and as we cuddled, realization dawned:

I'm not a virgin anymore!

I sighed and stroked a copper curl away from her face. This is what it felt like to be a man. I heard people say that a warm glow of contentment flushed through their body, but this was the first time it had happened to me.

A bell pinged in the distance.

"Shit! Another customer!"

Kirsten bolted upright and hurriedly pulled the cups of her bra over her lovely pink nipples and began buttoning her blouse. I tried to help her off my lap but she sat on the horn again.

"Should I come out back?" A voice from inside the store.

"Just a minute!" Kirsten stepped off me and started walking back to the store, wriggling her skirt back down her hips as she went.

Not wanting to draw attention to myself I stayed in the car, awkwardly pulling up my shorts and my jeans. By the time I'd finished buckling my belt I heard Kristen's heels clicking toward me.

"He just wanted directions. He's gone now." She smiled at me whilst twirling a curl around one finger. "So... was that as good for you as it was for me?"

"That was, I mean you were, amazing," I said and I really meant it.

She patted down my jacket and fished out my phone.

"Ooo! You have the latest model!"

"Yeah I love my Aphone. Funny thing too, I went to school with the guy who designed it, you know, Marcus Goldenrod from Awesome Computers."

She pouted and took a photo of herself with it, then punched in a string of numbers. "He's pretty cute, but for an internet entrepreneur I'd pick you any day."

"I'm not a—oh, right."

She handed me back the phone which now had a number below her picture.

"Call me anytime, gorgeous."

Did she think I was gorgeous or that she was getting her hooks into a billionaire? She waved a portable credit card reader at me and I handed her one off the deck.

I lurched the car across the parking lot, struggling with the clutch, until I pulled up at the gates. Kirsten unlocked them and they swung open. She winked and waved her thumb and pinky by her ear.

"Call me!"

"Sure Kirsten."

I slid down my sunglasses and settled back in the racing seats as I pulled out into the street. Another wave of elation ran through me, relishing the knowledge that I, Johnny Johnson, age twenty-four, was no longer a virgin.

"I'm a man!" I hollered out to the whole wonderful world and was struck by the puzzled look two mustachioed men holding hands on the sidewalk gave me when I drove past.

Chapter 4: A Teacher Appears

11:52 am

I pulled out The List, laid it on the passenger seat and got out my pen. Two bold strikes and two more dreams fulfilled:

Number 5: Bone a hot redhead

Number 24: Drive a Porsche

Satisfaction.

Now. Where to do some more crossing off? I scanned The List. Where is the best place to find girls at, I checked my watch, almost noon? No clubs would be open for hours. That leaves... The Crazy Cuban Beach Bar. Yes! High rollers and hot chicks. Not my kind of scene. Not until today.

I dropped the bellhop a fifty figuring I'd better learn how to play the part, took a deep breath, then walked through the door. Latin beats from the live band greeted me and I made my way to the nearest bar. The Crazy Cuban was an open-air sprawling amphitheater of verandas, big party tables, small nooks for two, all wrapped around a kidney-shaped pool.

The pool was full of bronzed bikini babes, squealing and splashing each other. Well-heeled dudes lounged around with colorful cocktails in their hands admiring the girls and swapping jokes. I waved for the barman.

"What'll be?"

"Oh." I hadn't really thought this through. "A... um, a martini?"

"You say it like you aren't sure. Is there anything else I could fix you?"

"No, no, I'm sure. A martini would really hit the spot just about now."

"Vodka or gin?

"Um, vodka?"

"Shaken or stirred?"

What would James Bond do? "Shake—"

The barman narrowed his eyes and shook his head.

I swallowed the sentence and tried again. "Stirred?"

"Coming right up, buddy."

I sipped it as I scanned the place again. Any single ladies? Everyone was talking to someone or other. I felt out-of-place and as alone as ever. Focus man! Remember you're on the clock here. I took another sip then took the plunge.

A woman in her twenties, crop top and miniskirt, swayed in time to the music as she waited for her drink that was currently being tossed overhead in its shaker by the mixologist. I cleared my throat.

"Great party, huh? Do you come here often?"

"Beat it loser." She didn't even turn around.

Okay... I picked up my drink and headed for the pool. Two guys were laughing hysterically and one of the bikini babes was standing off to the side. Separated from the main herd. Like a prowling lion I made my move.

"Hey there beautiful, I'm Johnny—"

"Get lost, jackass."

I shaded my face and wheeled away. The olive on a cocktail stick suddenly demanded my attention and I focused on chewing it slowly, waiting for the red to fade from my cheeks. How the hell was I supposed to work through The List if I couldn't get a girl to talk to me?

I slumped in a chair and took a look around at everyone else enjoying themselves. And here I was, given a single day to enjoy myself before a terrible end. Maybe I really was a loser after all and I'd been hiding behind my micropenis as an excuse to avoid facing the truth.

The cloud that had been passing overhead parted and a shaft of sunlight descended, picking out in a highlight beam a sixty-something-year-old man seated near the bandstand. Lean and tanned, and his long silver hair swept back to fall around his collar. Wearing a dark grey suit and vivid open-necked purple silk shirt, surrounded by beautiful women of all ages, colors and sizes. They were laughing with him and all seemed to want to touch his arm or rest their hand on his shoulder.

He stopped laughing abruptly, and his piercing blue eyes scanned the bar, then locked onto me. Staring hard at me as if trying to make up his mind. He raised his hand and beckoned me over, and with a somnambulist's slowness I went to him.

The stare never wavered as I crossed the bar and when I arrived he nodded and gestured to a seat, which I took. He kissed the hand or cheek of each woman there and, despite their pleadings, bid them good day. He waved at the barman who responded with a nod and a thumbs-up.

"Hi," I said and I managed a weak smile, although I didn't really understand why I had come to his table.

"Your game is very weak is it not?" He had an interesting accent I couldn't quite place, and he tilted his head as he studied me.

"My game?" I had no idea what he was talking about.

"Yes, your game. The Game. Winning women's admiration, their lust, and ultimately bedding them."

"Oh *that* game. Yes, my game is very weak. I'm a total loser, and, although I can't believe I'm saying this to a complete stranger I only met thirty seconds ago, I only lost my virginity an hour ago. So yes, my game is weak, about as weak as it can possibly be."

He smiled and thanked the waitress as his drink arrived in a tumbler chinking with glass. She winked at him and left us.

"How the hell do you do that?" He was actually making me angry now and I felt my fingers close into fists.

"Ah," he said as he swirled his drink. "That is my game; I am playing it at a higher level than you."

"Well I'm on level zero so I guess anyone is at a higher level than me."

"No, friend. You are at level one because now you know there is a game. What's your name?"

"I'm Johnny"

He nodded slowly as if it mean something important. "And you now have a specific question you want to ask me, do you not?"

I pondered this until it dawned on me. "How do I get to a higher level?"

He laughed then took a drink from his tumbler. "Excellent, now it begins."

"Wait a minute are you about to give me a fucking training montage?"

"The Buddha said; when the student is ready, the teacher will appear. For you that time is now, and I am ready to be your teacher."

"At this point I'll try anything. What do I call you?"

"The Master."

"Seriously?"

"Yes."

"The Master?"

He nodded.

"Okay, I just hope none of the girls overhears me. They'll think we are gay lovers."

He fingered my lapel. "Do you have pants to match this fine jacket?"

"They're being altered now."

"Excellent, and..." He glanced at my worn sneakers and his lip wrinkled. "Burn those and buy something more suitable for a gentleman. Woman can learn a great deal about a man by the state of his shoes, and not without good reason."

"Dress tips? I think it is going to take a bit more than that to get me up to your level."

"Patience, young one. An artist paints in layers." He nodded at his tumbler, empty save the ice. I hadn't seen him finish it. He raised an eyebrow at me.

"Oh right! What are you drinking?"

"Italian Stallion. My signature drink. You should pick one too. Ordering unusual cocktails fascinates women."

"Noted. Are you Italian?"

He chuckled. "No, but I am a stallion. Now do you see how it works?"

"Heh. Also noted."

I waved at the same barkeep that had been so friendly to the Master but couldn't seem to get his attention. I walked over to the bar and made the order, and by the time I got back there was a leggy Latina in tight jeans, heels and a black bikini top. Her jeans were so low I could see a skinny pink thong above them, and she was beautiful; early twenties, ripe body, a poster girl for an illustrated dictionary laid open on the word 'sultry'. She leaned over the Master's chair and whispered in his ear. When I set the tumbler on the table he patted her on the ass and she left with a pout on her lips.

"Wow, you sure work fast, Master."

"I do, and someday you will too. Tell me Johnny, do you know what a peacock is?"

"That bird with the big purple tail?"

"Women are attracted to peacocks, Johnny. It is genetic. They can't help themselves but be drawn to the flamboyant. Lose the T-shirt and get something flashier when you buy your pickup shoes."

"Okay. Got it. Anything else besides how I dress?"

"That is just setting the scene. Now I need you to concentrate very hard on this next one. The very first thought that comes into your head will be wrong, but the words will be right. Are you listening?"

I nodded.

"Are you really concentrating?"

I nodded again.

"Everyone has already been told the single greatest thing any pick up artist can know. They have probably been told it so many times that it has become invisible to them. There are many things I can teach you that will lift your game, take you to higher and higher levels, but this is the golden truth. What is the most important thing to do when you approach a beautiful woman?"

I waited, feeling a tingling rise up my spine and goosebumps on my arms as he swirled his Italian Stallion and drained it in one go. He leaned on the table and pointed at me.

"Be yourself."

I groaned and slumped in my chair. "Seriously? That wasn't worth the price of the cocktail."

"Your first thought is wrong."

"What?"

"Concentrate, Johnny. Visualize approaching that beautiful Latina, see? She is even looking at us. Imagine walking up to her and introducing yourself. What would it be like?"

"I couldn't do that. She is so out of my league it's like she is from another galaxy, far, far away."

"What would happen, Johnny?"

"Well the first thing, before I even walked up to her I'd start sweating. Not regular sweating—I could win gold at sweating in the Olympics. I'd be drenched. Oh, and then the trembling, my hands would be shaking like a ninety-year old diabetic who'd taken too much insulin. Finally the stammering. It could take me a whole minute just to spit out 'hi', and just enough time for her to throw her drink in my face and walk away."

"You get all that, just from talking to a stranger?"

"Yup."

"But none of that happened when you talked to me, did it Johnny?"

"Yes but, but you're a guy. It's totally different."

"Why, Johnny? And before you answer take a moment to think very carefully about what I have said. This is a crucial turning point in your path." He tapped the rim of his glass with his index finger and I went back to the bar for him.

His words ran through my mind as I waited for his drink to be served. Be yourself? What kind of advice is that? It's useless is what it is. Maybe... I want to say that I had a lightning flash of revelation, but it was more like that warm glow you get when you are eating something that you didn't think had chili in it.

I set down the Master's cocktail in front of him.

"My answer is a question, Master."

He ran a fingertip around the edge of his tumbler and it gave off an ethereal ringing. "Yes, Johnny. What is The Question?"

"How do I be myself?"

He threw his head back and laughed, clapping his hands together. "Bravo, Johnny. Bravo!"

For the first time I felt like I was getting somewhere and my frustration faded into a strange kind of elation. It was like the first step out the house when you are going on vacation. You lock the door, pick up your bag, and you know, deeply, that you are leaving behind the old for the new. That was how I felt right then.

"You must learn two things, Johnny. Who do you want to be, and what it means to be that person. You were relaxed when you talked to me. Some guys wouldn't, they'd be nervous and uncomfortable, but not you. Think about guys that can talk to women and not get nervous. That is the kind of person you want to be Johnny, isn't it?"

"Yes!" I wanted it urgently, desperately and I could feel the yearning physically, gnawing at my guts.

The Master settled back in his chair and sipped his Italian Stallion. "The journey will take some time, but day by day you will find yourself getting better game and taking it to new levels."

I grabbed his jacket sleeve and pulled him toward me, my happiness splintering into shards of pain as panic set in. "Master, I don't have all that time. I don't even have a full day. Tomorrow morning a doctor is going to cut my penis off or I will die." I released his sleeve and cradled my head in my hands.

I heard him sigh, and then felt his hand resting on my forearm. "Johnny, I feel for you, I really do, but what I practice is science, not magic. I can't teach you all you need to know, right here, right now."

"I'm doomed—"

"But I can give you a crash course in the basics."

"Something that will work today?"

"Yes."

"Sweet!"

I spent the next hour hanging on his every word, oh and shuttling back and forth from the bar. Wow, the old guy sure had a high alcohol tolerance; he just packed them away without the slightest sign of inebriety. I took notes, scratched my head and nodded enthusiastically a lot. Eventually he nodded, pushed away his empty glass and stood up. He handed me his card which simply said 'The

Master' with his phone number underneath.

"It was a pleasure to meet you Johnny, and I wish you good fortune. You must begin the game immediately, go to her. Go to her now."

He pointed to the cute Latina from earlier and I knew she was out of reach to the old Johnny Johnson, but there was now a new me, or at least a 'me' I wanted to be and believed I could become. She danced in front of the band, slender brown arms above her head, tossing her hair around and wriggling her round hips. Damn it. Why did I find her exposed armpits such a turn on? The violin curve from her hip to her narrow waist started a pulsing in my pants and I saw the sheen on her body, glistening darkly in the hard line down the middle of her abdominals.

The bartender managed to hand me a fresh bottle of Mexican beer, but couldn't be bothered to open it. At least that was a problem I knew how to deal with, and with the amazing power of my wanking pinch grip I easily popped off the bottle top. I leaned back against the bar swigging the beer and tried to think how I would put the Master's words into practice. I felt several beers might be a wise start but I knew that wasn't the way and that it would be bad for my game.

The Latina had her back to the band, still dancing with her arms held high then she raised her head and caught me looking at her. I looked away, took a sip of beer, looked back. She walked toward me with a smile on her full red lips. Her wavy hair settled around her shoulders and she ran her fingers through it, pulling it damply away from her face.

"Hey cutie," she said. "I'm Raquel. I saw you talking with the Master. He a friend of your or what?"

"Actually I just met him, but I think he just changed my life. I'm Johnny, by the way."

She held her hand up as if showing off a ring. I checked, she wasn't wearing any, so I just shook her fingers and she laughed.

"He changed my life too. I was the most uptight bitch in the world until I met him. He just had this animal magnetism, I felt myself losing control and there was nothing I could do to stop it, and worse, I didn't want to stop it. And then there is the sex. *Dios*, he is amazing. He's not called the Master for nothing."

"He's quite a guy," I said weakly and took another slug of beer.

"Say," she said taking hold of my lapels and stepping closer to me, hot sweaty body and musky perfume occluding my senses. "I've been partying all night and I'm totally bushed. Wanna take me home and put me to bed?"

I choked on my beer and managed to put the trembling bottle down on the bar before I dropped it.

"Yes. Yes I do."

She slid her hand in the back pocket of my jeans as we walked toward the exit. The guys by the pool stopped their hyena cackling as we went past, peering over the top of their sunglasses and frowning. My heart hummed and my smile felt big enough to say hello to the sun. I was walking out of the coolest bar in town with the hottest chick it had to offer!

As we passed the Master's table Raquel called out her goodbye and I gave him a discrete thumbs up. He just tapped his temple with a one-finger salute then we were gone.

Chapter 5: The Latina

1:39pm

"Nice ride, honey."

Raquel tapped her address into the GPS and I pulled out into the traffic. She wriggled in the seat and yawned.

"Wooh I'm beat! Do you know how hard it is to get laid in this city? Twelve hours of clubs and bars and I only met jerks and deadbeats."

I sympathized with her and after a few minutes turned into a quiet cul-de-sac and pulled into her drive. Raquel got out the car even before I'd switched off the ignition. She unlocked the door, beckoned me in, then took me by the hand and led me upstairs.

Her bedroom had clothes strewn across the floor, chair and bedside table. There was a red brassiere hanging from the lampshade and the king-size was unmade. She whooped and swung me in a dancer's twirl so my legs hit the edge of the bed and I sat down abruptly. She straddled me, knees digging into the mattress and ground her jean-covered parts against mine. Her eyelids drooped and her moaning low, almost a growl. My heart beat so hard I could feel the pulse in my ears but it was nothing compared to the surging in my pants.

"So Johnny, you want me sweaty or showered?"

I struggled to breathe as she rocked against my hard-on and any delay was not on my mind, besides her voice was getting lower and she was talking slower and I didn't want her to fall asleep on me and blow my shot at her.

"Sweaty works for me—"

She chuckled and pushed my jacket from my shoulders, flung it over her shoulder and pulled up my T-shirt. Raquel tugged it free of my raised arms, balled it and tossed it away before pushing me back on the bed.

"I... Raquel..." I tried to speak but she raked her nails down my chest and across my stomach, leaving eight long pink weals in my skin. She unbuckled me and I placed my trembling hands on her waist. She was damp and hot and my palms felt electric as I caressed her slippery flanks.

"Do me," she said. "Harder, squeeze me, scratch me."

I slid my hands down her abdominals, hard and flat with the mesmeric nuance of her skin, running my thumbs down the vertical groove in the middle, then my nails down her flanks and back to her tummy.

"Yes..." She groaned and arched her back and I saw peaks forming under the black Lycra of her bikini top. She took my hands and placed them over her breasts. "Squeeze me Johnny, don't be gentle with me."

I didn't need to be asked again. Her boobs were bigger than Kirsten's and larger than my handful so I cupped them from different angles before tugging the bikini down. Her large brown nipples popped into view, stiff and erect like little fingertips and her dark areola were as wide as milk bottle tops. I rolled them between my fingers and she moaned, her head falling forward and her hair draping my hands. I tugged on her nipples and she stifled a small sound then collapsed on me biting my bottom lip and kissing me.

I gently ran my nails down her back and she growled her pleasure, starting to bite and suck at the side of my neck. She worked her way across my shoulder and chest, bit my nipple so hard that I squealed out and she sat up, chuckling at me, her hair trailing across her face. I had never been this turned on in my life and felt somewhere out of my mind to have this incredible female on top of me and smoking with desire.

"Can you satisfy me Johnny? I've been dancing for hours watching men lust after me and my pussy is burning."

"I'll try," was the best I came up with.

She climbed off me and my heart sank, thinking I'd blown it, but she reached behind her back, tugged, and the bikini came away. She held it in front of her between finger and thumb, then let it fall to the ground.

"Oops. It fell off..."

I gasped, and believe me, if you had seen her standing there like I did, you would have as well.

She slid her hands across her belly, over her boobs and licked her fingertips, circled her nipples with them, polishing their tips. She had absolutely no tan lines and I was intensely jealous of her sunbed.

"Do you want me, Johnny?"

My throat was so dry I could barely speak. "Yes," I croaked.

Raquel kicked off her shoes, one after the other. She unbuttoned her jeans and turned her back to me, slowly pulling her jeans past her hips, exposing her beautiful brown bottom, bisected by the pink stripe of her thong, stepped out of the crumpled legs and looked over her shoulder at me.

"Do you really want me, Johnny?"

My breathing was so shallow I thought I might pass out at any minute and I made some half-choked drowning noise, nodding my head.

"Take off your jeans then, dumbass."

"Oh! Right, on it." If you were asked to bet whether it was possible to remove a pair of sneakers, jeans and shorts in under five seconds you would probably bet no. I'm here to tell you that you'd lose.

Her thong was in her hand and she did the 'oops' thing again. I didn't mind the repetition.

"And the socks, Johnny."

"Done!"

Then she jumped me. She obviously considered the gentle nibbling that had gone on before to be light foreplay. I squealed as her teeth went into my neck and nails dug into my shoulders. I tried everything but I don't think she had ever heard of a safeword. She rubbed herself across my belly, sticky damp of her arousal, rubbed against my chest. She pinned my arms back with her shins, knees by my ears and I looked up at her musky lips, waxed with a dark Brazilian stripe.

"Do you like eating pussy, Johnny?"

I discovered over the next twenty minutes while she humped my face that I actually did. Although I was broadly aware of the principals involved, watching porn is no substitute for practice. Through trial and error I worked out what worked and elicited the most noise from Raquel, and I kept doing it. It was deeply arousing to taste her response to my stimulus and as twitches overcame her gyrating body and she panted in short bursts I wanted nothing more than her to come all over my face. She cried out to *Dios* and clamped my head between her beautiful buttery brown thighs and I knew I was right there in Heaven with Him.

After a few more shudders she relaxed her grip on my head then flopped over on the mattress.

"That was amazing. Oh wow. Now come over here and ride me. Ride me hard Johnny."

I clambered over to her, between her bent knees, positioning myself to enter her. She opened her hooded eyes with a lazy smile, then looked down my body.

"*¡Madre de Dios!* Is that thing real?" She bit her bottom lip.

"It's all Johnny..." Awesome—my first catch phrase!

"Be gentle, Johnny..."

Now she wants me to be gentle?

I slipped in the tip and her head dropped back with a sigh. Then I rode her and she pulled on my hips urging me deeper with each stroke, only her nails digging into my flesh kept me from blowing my load in seconds but as she begged me to go deeper, to go harder, her claws sank further into me. I entered a semi-conscious state of delirium watching this incredible woman writhe beneath me in ecstasy, an ecstasy I was creating in her, and my own sensations combined with the argent fire burning in my hips.

Riding along what seemed to be a white-tipped frothing wave carrying us along with it, she started to convulse and pant again then the wave crashed and broke and I came so hard my vision blurred, motes of dark light dancing in my vision. I slowly lowered myself to her and our sweaty bodies coiled and she mumbled her thanks languorously in my ear.

A deep drowsy glow came over me; my eyelids heavy and my breathing slow. I thought Raquel must surely sleep now, but after a few moments she rolled me off her and propped herself up on one elbow.

"Incredible, Johnny. You truly are one of the Master's students." She pecked the gentlest kiss on my cheek, then got up. I didn't want to miss the opportunity to watch her walking away so I forced myself awake and sat up.

I just caught a gratifying glimpse of her rear disappearing out the door, then a moment later heard the rush and gurgle of a shower. Hoping after what we just shared that I'd be welcome, I followed her.

The shower room was barely bigger than a cupboard and she smiled at me as I came in, lathering her hair with shampoo, reminding me of watching her dance at the bar. She held my gaze as she reached for the shower cream and spread it over her breasts, across her belly, between her legs. My heart rate started rising as she teased me.

"*Dios.* Does that thing never go down?"

I glanced at it, pointed at her soapy tanned lusciousness like some kind of gun dog, then shrugged. "Guess you just have that kind of effect on me."

She rinsed and turned off the water, drawing a towel across her back as I ogled the rest of her drip drying. She wrapped it around herself and stepped out. I reached for her and she swatted my hands away.

"Uh-uh. Not when I've just got clean. Take one yourself and we'll see about a rematch."

Standing under the hot water I smiled. After all my years of hurt, things were starting to go right for me. Spectacularly right. Raquel-right. And Kirsten-right. If I was going to go out, then I was going to do it in a blaze of glory. Just like in those gladiator movies. Today is a good day to die. Why was I being so brave? All these endorphins were probably making me crazy but I was liking it and I wanted more.

I sauntered back to Raquel's bedroom with a towel around my

waist. I heard her laugh then she called out to me.

"Who is Gwen Hertzensbrecher, Johnny? An old girlfriend?"

Her towel was on the ground and she was draped naked across the bed, reading a small piece of paper.

The List! Oh my God, she's going to think I'm a pervert and kick me out!

"You read The List? It's... it's private..."

She looked up, then she smiled. "You're a very organized naughty boy, aren't you? Tell me, why are so few crossed off?"

My heart sank. I didn't want to blow my chance of seconds with her, but I couldn't bring myself to lie to her. So I told her the truth. Well, part of it.

"Well, the truth is yesterday I was a virgin."

"You're full of shit!"

"No I swear, it's the truth. I lost my virginity this morning and now I'm seeing if I can make any of my dreams come true."

"But Johnny, why today? What held you back all these years?"

I sighed. "Raquel, I always just thought I was a loser, I was unpopular at school, and I guess at some time, well, I just stopped trying." Great, now I looked like a loser in front of her.

She got up from the bed and gave me a naked hug, and just the feel of her glorious boobs pressing into my chest made me feel whole lot better.

"Kids can be really cruel Johnny. Just put it behind you. Here, there is another one you can cross off your list."

I looked at the paper and her thumb marked Number 7. I got out my pen and struck it off.

~~Number 7: Pound a hot Latina~~

"Doesn't that make you feel better, Johnny?" She smiled encouragingly at me. "Now what's next?"

"What do you mean?" I said.

"The list, what do you want to do next?"

"Well, I thought seeing as we are both here, and naked, we could—"

"No, no, no! Be adventurous, be bold! Here, what about this one?"

I looked where she was pointing, and I can't lie, a shiver of excitement ran through me. On The List it said:

Number 11: Have a threesome

Raquel rubbed the small of my back with one hand and toyed with my nipple with the other. My towel slipped from my waist and folded horizontally over my erect cock.

"Raquel, are you saying that you'd be into that?"

She kissed my neck. "Let me call a friend, gimme a minute."

Raquel wriggled delectably across the rumpled sheets and reached for her phone on the bedside table.

"Hey Angel, how you doing sweetie? ... Yeah fine, fine, actually better than fine, just finished rolling with an *amazing* guy... oh yeah, you'd definitely be into him... okay cool! See you in a minute!"

She hung up and rolled back on the bed, running her fingertips across her belly and smiling at me. "Two minutes, stud-muffin. Angel only lives across the street."

My heart thumped like it was doing 200bpm. I didn't think you could get that excited about someone who wasn't even in the same room as you. I grinned at Raquel who laughed back at me and raised her arms up to welcome me. I fell onto her hungrily, kissing her on those full, juicy lips, then moving down to her neck, her collarbones, the slopes of her breasts, her nipples that darkened and swelled under my ministrations.

The doorbell rang.

Raquel squealed and wriggled out from under me, wrapped her towel around herself and trotted out the door. I lay back with a sigh and lazily stared at the ceiling as a contented floppy grin formed on my face, breathing deeply and slowly and savoring the moment. What a great day this was turning out to be after all.

I could hear voices downstairs, indistinct, but burbling happily. I sat up.

One of the voices was very deep.

I crept to the door and peeked down the stairs.

Raquel was holding hands with a tall dark man who had a very thin, sharply outlined goatee. His black T-shirt was stretched tight over broad shoulders and bulging pecs.

Oh God. Oh God. Oh God. Angel is a dude.

My heart took off like a locomotive and I panicked. What the hell was I going to do?

Remember the bet about how fast I could get my clothes off? I think I beat that record going the other way. Damn the socks I could leave them behind. The window—the damned window had a security lock! I darted around, overturning the trash she had piled up on the window sill, but no key.

The rumble of speech from downstairs stopped. I was out of time. My brow was starting to glisten with sweat and I reached for the tab on the security lock with my masturbation pincer grip, flexing the cords in my wanking arm, gritting my teeth as I applied torque. It slowly began to bend then tore away like the tab on a can of soda. I was already hanging from the window frame when I heard them coming up the stairs. By the time they got to the bedroom I was in the car and firing the ignition.

"Johnny? Johnny, honey? Where are you?"

"Hey dude, I'm Angel. Raquel said you like to party. Where are you hiding, dude?"

This was not on The List.

Raquel leaned out the window, she dropped her towel and I had a final look at her glorious tanned globes. "Where the hell are you going *pendejo*?"

"Come back, dude! Be open-minded, you might like it. I promise

I'll be gentle!"

The engine roared, the tires squealed, and I was out of there. The virginity of my bottom thankfully intact. I drove fast, weaving between cars, taking turns at random until my pulse had slowed enough for me to think clearly.

I pulled over, let out a long sigh, then got out The List and made an amendment.

Number 11: Have a threesome *with two girls*

Better. Unambiguous. Know what would be even better? Keep that hidden, bozo. There was no telling what would happen if this got into the wrong hands.

Chapter 6: The Coffee Shop Girl

2:57 pm

I slumped against the steering wheel, gripping it loosely and resting my forehead on the finely perforated leather arc. I felt so exhausted I didn't think I could go on. The roar and blare of the traffic seeped through my sleepiness and something approaching wakefulness returned.

I couldn't sleep now, not today, not tonight, I had to make the most of every hour.

I needed coffee.

There was a great place I used to go to when my internet was down and I needed to mooch some free wifi. I walked in to the relaxing murmur of quiet conversations, the aroma of freshly ground and roasted beans, the hiss of the machines. Enzo's Books and Beans was that perfect mix of a haunt for locals combined with the smooth running of a larger chain store. Enzo himself was actually a Russian émigré called Vassily, but he was really set on the whole Italian theme and had black and white posters of scenes from The Godfather on all the walls.

There were round tables with chrome framed sit-up chairs near the counter, battered and worn brown leather couches further back. Two rows of bookshelves divided up the ground floor and a cast-iron spiral staircase went up to another section of books.

I ordered, thinking that you really ought not to need to take a breath break in the middle of a coffee order, then a couple of minutes later retreated with my frothy mug and a large BLT sandwich to the furthest corner of the coffee shop. There was a single seat recliner, under the shadow of an old air conditioning unit, now home to posters for local bands. Collapsing in the chair I let my legs go floppy and sipped my coffee with closed eyes, savoring the milky chocolatey goodness.

The faces of Felicia, Kirsten and Raquel danced in my mind, and other body parts as well, and I smiled as the first welcome tickles of caffeine started to tease at my nervous system. In that peaceful moment I felt at one with the world and even my situation. True, I was either going to die tomorrow or suffer a fate just as bad, but damn it I was going out with a bang, or in fact a series of them. If this was to be my destiny then I wanted to end my twenty-four years of loserdom in a sexual supernova of epic proportions.

I smiled and opened my eyes meeting the gaze of someone who quickly looked away. It was woman of about twenty, dark russet hair with a hint of purple to it that was tied at the back but had a long fringe. Under the fringe were a pair of thick framed glasses and between them they practically masked her. She had no makeup on that I could see and wore a plain knee-length brown dress with an oversized brown sweater on top. The old army boots with several inches of hiking socks poking out the top completed her dress-down ensemble.

She peeked at me over the top of the book she was browsing then turned away when she saw me watching her. On any other day I'd have been trembling to find a girl looking at me, going through that horrible deja-vu of hoping she'd like me and knowing it would end up in a micropenis train wreck. Or a micro train wreck. Or something with the metaphor of tiny objects trying to enter a tunnel and failing spectacularly. Today I didn't have that concern, but I didn't have much time.

I checked The List. No... no... nope. No geek-related list items. Sorry sister, not today.

I looked up and she was checking me out again. Just as quickly she buried her face in the book. Then I saw the cover text.

EXTREME SEX: Beyond the Kama Sutra

Okay maybe not a completely meek geek. Maybe she was the kind to take off her glasses and let down her hair, going from Plain Jane to Sexy Suzy to the surprise and pleasure of the hero. She slammed the book closed and banged her forehead against it a couple of times then stamped a booted foot. She marched over to me, roses forming on her cheeks, and took a deep breath.

"You have one thick leg and one thin leg," she said.

"Excuse me?"

She covered her face with one hand while the blush ran down both sides of her neck.

"I meant to say 'hi'," she said, somewhat muffled behind the hand.

"Oh right," I said. "That's an easy mistake to make."

"Sorry, I'm such a klutz. I'll leave you alone now."

Her shoulders slumped and something in this cold-hearted player's heart melted. I remembered being on the other side of conversations like that. It wasn't nice, screwing up your courage, expecting a brush off, then hating yourself for the rest of the day for being such a dork.

"What's your favorite movie?" I said.

"Huh?" She looked up, her lips parted. I reevaluated my Plain Jane assessment, now at closer range and decided she was definitely a fixer-upper. As long as her reading habits were consistent.

"Movie. Favorite. Yours?"

"Avatar I guess. Or maybe Casablanca."

"Wow, that's quite a spread."

She shrugged, her usual pale color was returning as the blush faded away. "Yeah but people always say Casablanca when you ask them, don't they?"

"I don't know, I've never seen it. I'm more of a book person."

"Me too!" She skipped on the spot and then ahem'd. "Sorry about that. I get a bit shrill when I get excited. I guess that's why you're here in the bookstore then, right?"

"Sure, why not. What're you reading?"

The blush was back with a vengeance and she screwed her eyes up. "I was just... I meant..."

"Hey, hey, it's okay. Really. I'm was just teasing you."

"It's not nice to tease people."

"Even when you're just breaking the ice?"

She opened one eye. "Were you?"

"Yes! Come on, sit down and tell me your name." She smelled faintly of peppermint as she passed me. I took a chug of coffee as it was starting to get cold and I knew I needed every drop of lovely caffeine in there.

"I'm Madison. Madison Swallow."

Foam frothed through my nose as I started choking. I reached for a napkin and as I wiped my face I heard her giggle.

"You did that on purpose Madison."

Her smile was pretty cute, I had to admit. Maybe her nose was a teensy bit big, but the smatter of freckles across it made it adorable as a whole.

"Maybe. I just wanted to see your reaction. You can tell how dirty someone is by the way they react to my surname."

"Oh, so now you know me?"

She nodded vigorously. "Yes, you're probably a sex fiend or some other kind of pervert."

"Woah, that's laying it on a bit strong, isn't it?"

"Oh, it's okay," she said. "I'm a pervert too."

I put down my coffee mug. "You aren't going to let me finish this are you?"

"Maybe... it depends.

"On what?"

"On whether you're going to come back to my apartment with me."

"Wow. Really? Just like that?"

"Mmm-hmm." She had stopped blushing entirely and was now peering at me through the thick-framed glasses and the gaps in her fringe.

What did I have to lose? I checked my watch.

"It can be as quick or as slow as you want it to be," she said.

"Okay... no, I mean, yes! Why not? We're consenting adults aren't we? You are consenting aren't you?"

"I'm inviting."

Her smile was growing on me and there was something in the way she looked at me that made me think I'd be missing out on a treat if I passed up on her. I decided she was, inviting that is. Ah heck; she was adorkable.

"I'm Johnny. Johnny Johnson."

"Sounds like there's a story right there."

I shook my head. "Sadly not as funny as yours. You want to go now?" I motioned toward the door.

She pointed at my mug. "Finish your coffee; you're going to need all your energy."

I laughed and drained the mug, patting away the foam moustache. There had to be a funny side to this. I set out today to pick up girls and now I was the one being picked up.

We walked out together and I pointed my keys at my car, which was parked in the space I'd found so conveniently directly outside the coffee shop.

"Shall we drive?" I beeped the remote and the car's lights flashed.

"That's your car?"

"Yup." I beamed at her.

"Oh. My. God," she said.

"Pretty cool huh?"

"I love it!"

"Yeah it's pretty awesome isn't it?" I was kinda getting off on the adulation and relishing being the big man.

She clenched her fists and bounced on the spot. "I love red cars! They're my favorite!"

"It's a Porsche..." I scratched my head.

She shrugged. "I don't really know much about cars but red ones are my favorite. Oh look! Another one!" She pointed at an old Nissan station wagon smoking and spluttering its way down the street. "If I ever get a car it'll definitely be a red one."

I kinda sagged. "So... should we go?"

"Nah, my place is just two blocks away. It's quicker to walk than to circle around looking for another parking spot."

She took my hand and led me down the sidewalk, our clasped

fingers swinging as we walked. She looked down at our hands then up at me.

"This is nice," she said, and I felt that it was.

Her block was an old oppressive concrete slab from the Fifties, but so many of the balconies had potted plants trailing from them as if nature was slowly asserting its claim. As we waited for the elevator to come down Madison kept sneaking glances at me then looking away.

She squeezed my hand.

When we reached her floor she headed down the corridor and unlocked room 327.

"Here we are! Make yourself at home, while I... slip into something a bit more comfortable." She giggled again and left me alone in her living room.

Two couches placed at right-angles took up most of the space of the small room. A ceiling height bookshelf covered one entire wall, books jammed in horizontally in any available space that was left. She had a big-screen TV on a wide cabinet that was stuffed with movie box sets, collectable series and director's cuts.

Oh, and then there were the stuffed animals. Noah could just have floated this room and been done with it in one go. She had lined them up along the backrest of the sofas, stuffed small ones into crannies between books and clustered a mountain of them behind the TV that loomed over the room, threatening to deluge an unlucky soul in plushy, Technicolor fluff.

She called from another room. "Be just a minute!"

I knelt on one knee in front of the TV cabinet to peruse her collection, brushing aside some more stuffed wildlife. One section appeared to be a homage to Joss Whedon, but down the other side was a collage of flesh colored tones. The spines read things like "Ass Rammers IV", or "Chained and Loving It 3", and "Slave Seduction 12: The Punishing".

With trembling hand I slid one out. On the cover was a blindfold naked guy, kneeling with his arms chained to a ring on the floor. Standing over him was a woman in stiletto heeled thigh-high boots and brandishing a whip with intent.

"There you are."

I slammed the case back in the cabinet, swept the plushies back in place, and my hand closed about a cylindrical object. I stood up, the words 'I can explain' and 'this isn't what it looks like' forming in my mind, then my jaw just flapped open.

Madison was wearing a one-piece latex bodysuit. When I say one piece that doesn't include the nipple holes and the fact that it was crotchless. Her stiletto-heeled boots had her looking down at me, having lost the thick framed glasses, from a vantage point of several inches and she had a long curly blond wig on her head, although some strands of her dark auburn were visible underneath. The slut-red lips and stick-on eyelashes kind of suited her though.

She smiled, but not the wholesome toothy grin from the coffee shop. This one was lopsided and lecherous, and I realized that I was afraid.

"You found The Beast, then. Good, I thought he'd been lost to us." Her voice was much lower

I looked at my hand and saw I was holding a black dildo, over a foot in length and as thick as a baseball bat.

"Madison, I can explain—"

"Silence slave. You will speak only when asked a direct question, and when you do you will address me as Madame Pain. Do you understand?"

She took a step forward and cracked a whip beside my ear. It was black and made from multiple leather straps.

She waited as I trembled in front of her, then winked at me and whispered, "It was a question; you're allowed to answer."

"Umm... I understand, sort of?"

She cracked the whip again and I flinched. She chuckled in the low tone she was affecting. "On your knees slave!"

She raised the whip and I fell to my knees before she had a chance to use it. Her legs were spread wide and I followed the black seams on the inside of her thighs to the opening between her legs. She was waxed completely bare; her labia engorged and pink, a silver ring gleaming on each side.

"Well done, slave. If you continue your obedience you will be rewarded. Now follow me to the dungeon."

Dungeon?

Madison, or rather, Madame Pain, swiveled on one heel and strode into the next room, her hips swaying as she took each step, and

I shuffled after her on my knees.

It was a bedroom, as cramped as the living room, with a single bed on each side, separated by two bedside cabinets that described the only remaining width of space. The left side of the room had posters of guys in black T-shirts with long hair making various signs with their hands. Skulls were a popular motif on their shirts, and the bed sheets were crumpled to the side, a pillow half wedged in the corner. The other side of the room had posters of clean-cut smiling boy bands and the pillows were edged with lace, the sheets drawn tight like a hotel maid had just finished with them.

Madame Pain wiggled her whip at that side of the room and hissed softly at me. "My roomie's side of the room. Stay out of it."

I nodded, feeling a lightheaded dizziness at the surreal situation.

"Onto the bed, slave. And be quick about it."

She pointed at the messy bed and I crawled over and clambered onto it. Taking the handle of the whip in both hands, she flexed it while examining me from head to toe. The handle creaked as she bent it.

"Now, slave. Strip."

As she said it she spread her legs a bit further apart and thrust her hips forward, giving me a clear view of her pussy. I knew for a fact that I didn't have 'Fuck a girl with piercings' on The List, but the pulsing in my pants made me wish I had. I kicked off my sneakers, hung my jacket on the foot post and slung my T-shirt over it.

I felt a silly nervousness, but my arousal was taking over as I saw her watching me intently, the tip of her tongue moistening her lips. She was looking at my 'thick leg' and as I put my hand to my buckle she tweaked her nipple and a shiver ran through her body.

Hell yes. This was going to be fun. I wriggled out of my jeans and they hit the floor, followed my shorts. Unbound, my cock stood to attention.

"OH!" Madison squealed shrilly, her hand clapping over her mouth, then she cleared her throat and Madame Pain took over again. "You have pleased me, slave. Now lie back and place your hands above your head."

I settled back, clasping my hands behind my head and waiting for her to climb on top of me. She grabbed my arm and twisted it and I heard a metallic clunk. I twisted my head and saw a pink furry bracelet on my wrist, chained to a matching bracelet on the bar of the head of the bed. Handcuffs? She twisted my other arm and before I could think further it was similarly restrained. I checked it out. This one was leopard patterned. Hooray for variety.

"Umm... Madison—"

She struck me across the chest with the whip and it was my turn to squeal. A swathe of pink stripes burned up across my skin, already tender from Raquel's raking.

"You will not speak unless it is to answer a direct question!"

I bit my lip and nodded.

"Now," she said. "Your intolerable behavior means you will not be rewarded. Instead, you will be punished."

My temperature dropped about twenty degrees and I suddenly felt very cold, naked and alone, chained to the bed of a crazy woman with a whip. I opened my mouth to plead to her that this had all been a terrible mistake but she glared at me and raised the lash so I clamped my jaw shut.

"How should I punish my slave, I wonder?"

She laid the whip across my throat and rummaged in a drawer in the bedside unit, but out of my line of sight. She came up with red candle and a Zippo lighter and I shrunk away from her. The lighter sparked and the candle flared.

Madame Pain placed her hand on my chest, stroking my whip marks, then traced one of Raquel's scratches from my nipple to my groin.

"So the slave has other mistresses? Interesting. Who deals with him the most severely, I wonder..."

She tipped over the candle and a blob of molten wax splashed onto my belly. My back twisted and I had an involuntary sharp intake of breath, expecting it to hurt more than it did. It burned for less than a second then a strange contracting feeling as it cooled, almost as if I had a warm thumb resting against me.

Madam Pain dropped more blobs, her smile growing broader each time I twitched, each little gasp. She held the candle over my cock, lying fat between my legs, and I shook my head vigorously. She closed her eyes and laughed in that low voice.

"Well it is no fun if the slave knows what is going to happen." She

"Ooo! You have the new one! Nope it's not ringing. Hang on where did I put mine? Oh, hey Vickie... mmh-hmm... yeah... not much, just breaking in a new slave... oh yeah, totally... pretty cute, when are you coming back? ... An hour? I don't think he'll last that long... yeah shame... okay honey later."

"Friend of yours?" I dared speaking with Madison around for a bit.

"Yeah my roomie, but I don't think she can make it back in time. Shame, you'd have loved her she's such a blast. Where is the camera button?"

"Hmm? Oh, the phone. They switched sides on this model, see?"

I heard the fake camera shutter noise, followed by a giggle.

"You look so cute like that!" The shutter went off a few more times in quick succession. "Why has it stopped working?"

"Please don't break my phone," I begged. "I love my Aphone, I don't know where I'd be without it..."

"That's what GPS is for. I'm putting my number in, what should I use for my profile pic? Oh I know..." There was another shutter-snap and she giggled. "It's kinda blurry so close up but my piercings look super cute! Anyway, where were we..." Madison left the building and the deep voice returned. "Yes, I remember, training the new slave."

I heard the crack of a bottle-top being flipped and felt a cool liquid trickling down my shaft. Hands closed around it and she began stroking it, a tantalizing light touch and the pulse ticked in me like a clock. I left out an involuntary moan.

"You see, slave? There can be pleasure as well as pain. Serve me well and you will be rewarded. If you want me to continue, you may thank me."

The alternating between fear and excitement, correction and gratification was making my balls ache and despite wanting to escape I also wanted release.

"Thank you Mistress Pain..." My cheeks burned at the humiliation and I started to move my hips in time with her strokes.

"But not too much pleasure, slave." She took her hand away and I groaned. "Roll over, now."

"But—"

I felt the strips of the leather whip being drawn across my quivering tip.

"Do you want me to whip you here, slave?"

I shook my head.

"Then do it."

I twisted in my shackles and managed to roll onto my front, or close enough. My arms were crossed with my face against them and my cock uncomfortably pinned beneath me.

"Have you heard of a paddle, slave?"

I thought of a canoe and could not possibly see a connection. "No, Mistress Pain."

There was a sharp crack and something hard impacted one of my buttocks. I cried out even as the paddle was lifted and a hot glow suffused my skin. The other cheek received a swift blow and I squealed again, only for the first buttock to receive another stroke. I was panting hard and despite being in such an awkward position my jumps at each paddle stroke rubbed me against the mattress and I was hardening again.

The rain of pain stopped and it sounded like the paddle had been placed on the cabinet beside me.

"Well done. You took your paddling like a good slave. You may turn around and receive your reward now."

Still breathing hard I twisted until I lay on my back. The bed creaked and shifted. Warm latex pressed against my hip and I felt her drag her other leg over me and assume a straddle position. My cock was resting against her belly, but I could feel the heat of her naked pussy against my balls. My cock twitched and she laughed.

"Are you ready for your reward now, slave?" She was sliding the lubricated underside of my cock across her latex suit, slipping it from side to side.

"Yes Mistress Pain."

Feeling like I might shoot at any moment, a ring was placed over my purple glans and a silicone sheath unrolled down my length. Her weight came off my thighs and her latex legs were on either side of my erection then she sank down on me, our groans in unison as we both felt the deep satisfaction of me hilting myself in her. She ground' herself in circles then lifted up so high I thought she was going to stop, but she plunged again and began to ride me like a pony.

I heard a whining, buzzing start then felt vibrations through her pussy.

"Oh mommy loves The Beast, yes she does."

She had stopped the rising and falling that let me slide in and out of her and had resumed grinding against me, stimulating herself with her vibrator and in my desperation I started bucking my hips to get some friction from her. My movements were banging The Beast rhythmically against her and she started to utter a chain of little shrill 'ooo-ooo' noises.

As she lost control I prayed that Madame Pain would be satisfied and safe little Madison would return, then she sank against my chest sighing quietly and I gasped as I was able to take deeper strokes, pulling against my handcuffs to pound deeper into her until a final thrill of pleasure hit me and I climaxed, shuddering with the intensity of it.

I think we must have dozed off for a bit. It was hard to tell how much time had passed, blindfolded and exhausted but the hazy, fuzzy treacle that my thoughts drifted through began to sharpen and I grew consciously aware of my surroundings. I could hear the traffic from the street, the soft snoring of the woman lying on me. I could feel the itchy tickly of the wig on my neck and against my cheek, and I could smell Madison's peppermint.

I rolled my shoulder, shrugging her off me, but she clung on and started mumbling. She wasn't a big girl but I struggled to roll her away with my manacled arms growing stiff above my head. Eventually she slid off to a louder protest and my wet cock slapped against my thigh.

"Hey wassamatter... oh! Hey you..."

The edge of my blindfold was tweaked up, I raised my head and Madison peered at me from under a mix of synthetic blonde bristles and her own fake dark red hair.

"Hi," I managed as I flinched slightly away from her, half expecting a slap or some more abuse.

"That was awesome," she said. "You were so much fun playing along. I loved it! Wasn't it great?"

I swallowed, choosing my words carefully. "You got it, Madison... now maybe it's time to untie me?"

She giggled. "Silly boy. That was just round one! You can't expect to go after just one round, can you?"

I yanked on my chains, despite the fur trims they bit into my wrists when I pulled that hard. "Please Madison, I've had enough fun for one day. Just take off these handcuffs, please?" I tried my best puppy dog face but my teeth were chattering and she still had that crazy lopsided smile on her face.

"No, no, no," she said wagging her finger from side to side.

She got up onto her knees and straightened her wig, "It's time for someone else to get their fill."

"What do you mean...?" Oh God, I don't like the sound of this.

She clambered over my leg and positioned herself between my legs. Madame Pain lifted up cock and held it straight up and started to tickle my balls. Second by second I relaxed, my shoulders loosening and my head fell back against the pillow.

"There, there little boy. We need to get you all nice and relaxed.

There..."

My cock dropped against my belly. There was a buzzing sound and I jerked my head up, one eye staring at her and my heart dropping through an abyss as I knew what I was going to see.

She had The Beast in one hand, more than twelve inches of vibrating, knobbly rubber, and in that moment it was the girth and not the length that scared me. I wondered why all these women were willing and eager to jump on my massive pole when I was so terrified right now.

"Please stop, don't do it!"

"First some romantic music, to properly set the tone."

She thumbed her phone and laid it down as the opening riff to *Slow Love* by Prince strummed out.

She held The Beast to her lips like a scary vibrating microphone and began to croon in time with the song.

"Don't take me dry...

Just take your ti—iime.

Use the KY...

Until it shi—iines..."

She leered at me and held The Beast under my balls, making them rumble and bounce. "It's not up to me, slave. The Beast has its own dark desires, and they must be satisfied." She pressed the rubber tip against my rectum and I clenched as hard as I could.

"Please Madison! It's me, Johnny! I don't want to play this game anymore; please stop!" I had tears in my eyes as I shook against the chains, pulling on them to drag myself further from her. I squealed as she twisted the huge vibrating dildo against me, the tapered tip beginning to spread my sphincter. "Please for the love of God stop..." I collapsed into a wailing mess, unable to keep fighting.

The Beast was withdrawn.

Between great racking sobs and deep breaths I slowly composed myself. Madison unlocked the handcuffs and I lay there, naked and cold, rubbing the red rings on my wrists. She slid the blonde wig off, and replaced her glasses from their resting place on the cabinet. She sat quietly looking at her hands.

"Weren't you ever having fun? I was only playing, you know."

My breathing was slowing to normal and I looked across at her, her head bowed and her bottom lip trembling.

I swung my legs off the side of the bed and stretched my back. "Hey, Madison, it's okay, don't cry. It's just that... well it was a bit intense. I'm not used to stuff like this. I was a virgin yesterday, if you can believe that."

Her genuine smile was the one I was attracted to at the coffee shop. "You mean I was your first? How cute!" She clapped her hands.

"Uh, no, actually..." How many was it? "You are like the fourth... or third and a half. I'm not sure. Tell me, if a virgin gets a blowjob, is he still technically a virgin?"

She shrugged. "I dunno, I guess so. Wait. You've had sex with four girls *today*?"

I wasn't sure how I felt about that right now. On one hand I thought I was awesome, but if someone didn't know my complete circumstances they might think I was kind of a douche.

I rubbed the back of my neck which was feeling unaccountably hot. "The thing of it is, well, ah heck, everything is happening so fast I can barely keep up, but it is kind of one of those 'last chance to try before I die' things."

She looked at me for a long time, I hoped weighing me between the awesome and the douche, then she put her hand on my knee.

"When my dog got old, and it couldn't really walk properly, and it pee'd around the house and couldn't help itself, well, my mom told us that she was going to take it to have it put down. She said that Pepe's quality of life was going to get worse by the day and that it was the kindest thing to do to ease his suffering. And I was really sad because Pepe was my best friend and I loved him, but on his last day I took him to all his favorite places, and played all his favorite games and when Mom came to take him away he looked so happy."

She had tears on her cheek and she wiped them away. I covered her hand on my knee with my own.

"Johnny, is what happened to Pepe happening to you?"

"I guess, something like that..."

She kissed me on the cheek, gently, then gave me a squeeze across my shoulders. "Then you should enjoy yourself as much as you can while there is still time." Madison stroked back a strand of hair that had been plastered to my forehead with cold sweat. "I'm sorry that... I... wasn't good enough for you..."

"No, Madison! You were, I mean you are great. You are an incredible woman..." She smiled that smile again. "Radiant—"

"You think I'm radiant? No-one has ever called me radiant before. Geeky, sure, but not radiant..." she punched me playfully on the chest. "You're alright, Johnny. You know that?"

I grinned back at her. "I guess so. Does that mean I'm free to go, Madame Pain?"

She blushed and put an arm across her bare nipples and drew her legs tight together. "You can't call me that when I'm out of character. It embarrasses the heck out of me. I'm just Maddie now; I'm not as tough as *she* is."

"Okay, Maddie." I rescued my clothes and dressed. I needed to wash but I also wanted to get out of here while I still had the chance, and didn't feel like risking some crazy shit if I asked to use her shower.

There was an awkward silence after I put on my jacket where we couldn't look each other in the eye.

"Okay, I got to be going. See you around Madison."

"Maybe bump into you at the coffee shop some time?"

"Maybe."

As I closed her apartment door behind me I breathed a long sigh. Some of it was relief, but some of it was this strange feeling that if things had been different I might have stuck around and got to know her better. With the other girls I'd simply been riding the locomotive of lust, powered by passion. Despite my abject terror for most of the time I'd been with her my mind kept getting drawn back to those first moments in the coffee shop; the cute shy girl with the dirty mind.

Chapter 7: Dodge Mrs. Robertson

5:06 pm

I walked back to the car and checked The List. Both sides. There had to be something here I could cross off... Damn it. Looks like I never had drunk fantasies about getting assaulted by someone with split personality disorder. And also weird that she was the first person I felt some kind of connection with. What does that say about me?

The Porsche was getting easier to handle and I even managed a couple of fingertip waves to girls that checked me out and giggled. Had it really been this easy all along? I slowed as I approached my apartment block, ready to swerve away if danger reared its head, but it looked like the coast was clear. This was always the riskiest moment so I pulled into another space conveniently in front of the door and jogged inside.

Throwing down Porsche keys on the counter, sticking my Aphone on charge and watching it light up with a photo of Madison's pussy, and heading for the shower after random sex with a beautiful stranger. All these things made it feel like I was the stranger, intruding on the insular, isolated life of the ghost of the old Johnny who'd lived here alone.

As I showered, a Zen-like clarity shaped my thoughts. I was totally accepting of the fact that this would be my last day on earth. I accepted that the micropenis loser was gone forever, and for the briefest moment I was who I was right now, and that right now was all we ever have. Who made me the loser? I saw now that it was me, not the micropenis. I made myself become that person, day by day, choice after choice. A hundred decisions a day that could have been different. Every day a chance to start again, but every day falling deeper into the rut I furrowed for myself.

I forgave myself, wholly and without prejudice, and gave myself permission to live to the fullest what little time I had left. I had never laughed and cried at the same before, and before that moment I wouldn't have known what that meant, but as my tears fell beneath the streaming shower I had never been so happy and free in my life.

It was a new Johnny Johnson that toweled off in front of the mirror. The eyes that examined me were wiser, kinder. I knew what I wanted to do. It was no longer me who needed to be happy—I wanted to make other people happy. And if they were hot chicks then that was just dandy.

Habit made me glance out the window before I left and my heart froze as I saw Mrs. Robertson waiting outside and talking to the Indian woman whose name I always butchered. Damn it! I always got the first six syllables right then lost my way. Those two could keep going for an hour and I didn't have any time to waste.

Chapter 8: Officer Degrady

The backdoor for my apartment meant climbing out the window and taking the rusty fire escape stairs. The alley was a narrow gap between my block and the next and only dumpsters lurked in the gloom that never saw sunlight. I'd just dropped to the ground when a dark sedan blocked off the exit from the alley and its headlights flashed twice.

The door opened and a cop got out, smoothing back her blond ringlets before placing her hat on her head and tugging down the brim. I couldn't see her expression, shaded behind black sunglasses, but she flashed a big torch into my face, the butt resting casually on her shoulder, and her other hand lightly gripping a truncheon at her belt.

"Hold it right there, perp." She had on more lipstick than I expected from a uniformed cop, but her lips were drawn thin and tight.

"Perp? I think there has been some confusion officer... officer?"

"I'll ask the questions here. Yes, you fit the description. You just burglarize that place?" She took the beam from my face and danced it around my open window.

"What me? No! I live there, you know, it's my apartment."

"So what were you doing climbing out the fire escape instead of just using the elevator?"

"Well I just... it's just I—"

"Okay perp, I'm going to need to search you, then call it in to see if you have priors."

"Wait what? Priors?"

"Up against the wall. Hands where I can see them. Spread your legs... spread 'em!"

She knocked the shaft of her torch against the inside of my knees until I was spayed as far as my jeans would let me, balancing against wall with my palms on the rough bricks.

"No funny moves, perp."

Her hands moved over my hip pockets, around my belt, patting down my jacket. She paused, then reached in a pocket, then pulled her hand out. She let out a long low whistle.

"The description was right, perp. Looks like you're the dealer we've been trying to catch."

My whole body jerked and I almost started to run right there. I twisted around, but she pushed me back to the wall. She dangled a plastic baggie filled with a fine white powder where I could see it.

"What! That's not mine!"

"That's way too much for any judge to take as personal possession. You're going to be tried as a dealer. Fifteen years minimum, perp. Twenty-five if you have priors."

I was breathing so hard but still felt out of breath, why was I getting set up? Had one of the girls today left it with me? Accident? On purpose?

"Officer, I swear I've never seen that stuff before. I've never done drugs!"

"They all say that. You can tell it to the judge. You know what they do to pretty boys like you in prison?"

She twisted one arm down behind my back and I winced as my shoulder wrenched. The cold steel snapped around my wrist then it was cinched painfully tight. The other arm was brought down just as cruelly and a second later I was cuffed. She pushed on my shoulder to turn me around and tipped up the brim of her hat with one finger as she brought her phone up to her ear.

"Reckon I'll be able to clock out early today. The chief always loves it when we bring in a dealer."

Sweat beaded on my lip and I knew my pale skin and trembling would just make her think I was guilty. There had to be some way to reason with her.

"I can prove I'm innocent, that it was my apartment. You can check, can't you? My keys are in my pocket. Surely that proves it?"

"It proves nothing, perp. You could have picked them up when you burglarized that poor guy's house. Now let me call the station, nothing personal, just doing my job."

As she flipped through the address book of her phone, I felt all my dreams melting away from me and I sank to my knees, my head bowed as I realized that I was going to spend my last futile hours in a police cell, waiting for a lawyer who probably wouldn't even arrive until after I was dead.

"Please, I'm begging you—literally on my knees begging you. There has to be some way to fix this. Some way to work it out..." My chest heaved as I tried to hold back the bawling that threatened to break out.

"Well..." The rigid authority in her voice gave way to a tremor. I seized that moment.

"Anything! Please God, I'll do anything..."

She lifted up my chin with butt of her torch, and I searched to see if I could see past those black sunglasses to a shred, even a trace of humanity there.

"Well... I'm feeling pretty horny. Very horny in fact. Reckon if you might satisfy me a bit, I might be prepared to look the other way, this one time, you know?"

The panic left me, replaced by dizzy confusion as I blinked dumbly at her. What was going on?

She turned my face from side to side. "You have a pretty mouth, perp. But I guess you've heard that before, in prison maybe?"

There could only be one possible explanation. This roll I'd been on today, one girl after another falling into my lap; I'd become sexually irresistible to women. They were completely helpless, driven by base animal urges making them desire me, hunger for me, need me. I had become what every man dreams of and that knowledge rose up in me like a volcano.

I closed my eyes and smiled, I wanted to spread my arms wide, embracing the world, but unfortunately the handcuffs restrained me, so I leaned my head back, beaming at the uniformed woman who was powerless to resist my charms. Moving my gaze from her feet to her face I'd noticed in passing that her high-heeled, knee-length black boots seemed to not quite meet regulation dress codes. Also, I couldn't recall the last time I'd seen a police officer in a black mini skirt instead of slacks. Her black blouse only buttoned halfway up and her pink see-through bra that restrained a generous cleavage was very visible.

She stepped closer to me and lifted the front of her skirt revealing that she had also omitted her regulation-dress-code panties, and her pubic hair had been trimmed into a small heart shaped patch that was much darker than the golden ringlets on her head.

"Do you like eating pussy?"

I knew the answer to this one now. "Yes, yes I do."

"Then lick me good, perp."

She straddled my shoulders and pressed her mound to my face. She had both hands on my head, clutching my hair and grinding against me. As I sucked her most sensitive spot she half pulled away, my tongue traced up from the top of her boots then across the satin skin of her inner thighs. Her buttocks bunched together hard and she pressed back against my lips. I lapped at her and she gasped.

"Slowly... slowly..." She pushed my forehead an inch away from her groin and I blew onto her clitoris. She breathed heavily and her head lolled forward, blonde curls falling over the silver badge pinned over her breast.

My tongue painted a groove, slowly licking up and hovering for a second on her button before beginning another long lick. She cooed and mumbled to herself and with each lick I imperceptibly increased the tempo.

"Yes... yesss..."

She rolled her hips so I could start each lick from lower, delving deep into her and my nose rubbing past her swollen button. My face was slick with her juice and I reveled in it; the control she had over me, just moments before, I now had over her. Except the handcuffs which were kind of an irritation as my arousal consumed me and I wanted to stroke and to squeeze her.

She started to twitch, a tight gasp preceding each spasm then let out a long moan as she shuddered through the top of her orgasm. She moved her pussy away, cradled my head against her hip and I waited as her breathing slowed.

"Well officer, am I free to go?"

She pulled my head back by my hair and stared at me. I wondered what color her eyes were. With the tension gone from her face she looked beautiful. She rolled her lips as she regarded me.

"Stand up."

I did so.

"Turn around."

The cuffs came off, one after the other, and I turned back to face her, rubbing my wrists. I opened my mouth to speak but she pushed me back against the wall.

"You haven't cleared your name yet."

I raised my hands to protest my innocence and she launched herself at me bruising my lips with her own, tasting herself on me. She ran one hand through my hair and the other rubbed its way across my chest, down my belly and to the bulge in my pants that thrilled to meet her touch. She gasped when she touched it, pulling back from me, tapping her lip with her finger.

"Maddie was right—it's massive!"

Maddie? What was going on?

Her fingers tore my buckle open, yanked my jeans down and she oo'd as I sprung free.

"I need you in me, I need all of you in me."

Another foil wrapper fluttered to the ground. She turned away and lifted her skirt and backed her pale tushy into me. She was so wet that I slid straight into her in one long thrust and she shuddered. I took hold of her hips and began to pound into her and she made a soft grunt each time she took my full length, a soft '*oh*' of disappointment as I almost pulled out.

"Fuck me, fuck me you dirty criminal. Teach the law to this naughty cop."

She fell back against me, shuddering as she began to climax again and I clutched her to me, angling up into her, taking the strokes that I knew would push me over the edge then twitching and a gasp as the fireworks went off.

We stood there panting for a minute, letting our pulses return to normal, and after a while she teetered forward, stumbling steps, as she pulled off me. She swayed slightly as she pulled her skirt back down, her gaze on my stiff cock.

"Wow... that was... amazing... Doesn't that thing ever go down?" She took off her hat, which had been at an angle, and smoothed back some golden locks that had fallen across her face.

I checked myself out, veined and glistening and apparently ready for more action. "I guess not."

"Freaky. In a good way I guess. Anyway, I got to run, just thought I'd pay a call on you when your contact popped up." She folded her glasses into her hat and smiled at me.

"Uh, what? So are you arresting me or not?"

She giggled behind the hat, cheeky blue eyes seeing a joke I didn't get.

"I'm not a real cop, silly. I just like to dress up, you know, like Maddie does. Only different, oh, and not together, 'cause that would just be weird, 'cause we live together. But we tell each other everything, but we wouldn't, you know... together... eew."

"Not a cop..." Exhaustion washed through me, my knees so weak I had to lean, pants around my ankles, against the brick wall for support. The image of myself in a jail cell watching my final dawn rising behind a windows with bars across it slowly fading away.

"You might want to zip up," she said helpfully. "You know, in case a real cop shows up, although you never know what might happen if she was really horny too. Or him maybe, I guess, if you are into that kind of thing."

I quickly pulled up my pants and did my belt. "How... how did you find me?"

She held out her phone which I finally worked out at that point was not the police radio I'd assumed it was. There was a photo of a skinny guy, naked on a bed with fuzzy handcuffs chaining him down, and a scarlet silk blindfold over his eyes. It was captioned 'Wang Monster'.

"Maddie added us as connections for you on FriendBook! Now we can see where each other are on GPS, you know, and chat and stuff. You want one of me? Huh?"

I gaped silently at her, powerless to protest and she pressed herself against the bulge in my jeans as she fished around in my pockets.

"Wow. I really wish I had more time to ride that thing. I'm like so late for choir practice already."

She plumped up her boobs, making sure her shirt lapels were spread as wide as they would go then held an open-mouthed, lip-licking pose as she snapped a photo at arm's length.

"Cute! What do you think, huh?"

"Cute..." I agreed. "But what about the cocaine?"

"It's just sugar, silly. I mean really, it's like you've never role-played at all!"

I thought of all the little figures of elves and orcs I'd painted in the tabletop role-play shop, and then looked at the sexy cop costume and at the pretty blonde woman who'd just banged me in an alley. No, I decided. I had never role-played before.

She kissed me on the cheek. "Sorry, but I really need to run. See you around some time!"

Her car horn honked twice as she pulled away and I slid down the wall, elbows on knees and cradling my head in my hands. As I calmed down I went over that events, then I chuckled. What an ass. She was pretty hot and, oh, The List.

Number 13: Get my freak on outdoors

Sweet.

I checked my watch. Got to keep moving. Every second counts.

Chapter 9: Incoming Transmission

6:16 pm

The traffic was heavy as the commuter flow headed back downtown. Now I remembered why I liked to walk so much. Staccato stop, start, punctuated by air horns. The flow picked up and we started moving again, but just as I was shifting for second a tank truck heading the other way and already with wheels over the dashed line veered toward me. I swerved hard to avoid it, my squealing tires clearing a space that would only have taken a credit card between my wing mirror and double wheels higher than my head.

I continued my swerve into a bus stop, my heart hammering, palms slipping on the steering wheel. Idiot tanker driver. Probably half drunk. Phew. Okay, calming down.

My phone rang.

"Johnny! How's it going?"

"Master? Uh, well, just had a close call but pretty good actually. But, erm, how did you get my number?"

"Johnny. There is a deep and mystical bond between us. You don't need to concern yourself with petty devices like that."

"Oh, okay Master. Hey I got to tell you, some of these girls are crazy. I don't mean just a bit freaky, I mean I have absolutely no idea what is going through their minds."

"We're all a bit crazy, aren't we? Have you been using your lessons, Johnny?"

"Uh, not really. It's more like they've been falling out the sky on me."

"It's happening naturally?"

I thought about Maddie screwing up her courage before hitting on me. "I guess so. Maybe I'm learning to actually be myself."

The phone was silent for a while and I thought I'd lost his signal, but then he sighed. "Johnny, are you aiming high enough? The way of the pickup artist is not just to pluck low hanging fruit. You must strive for the rarest, most delectable blossoms. Do you understand what I am saying, Johnny?"

I did. Remember buddy, go out like the supernova.

"Yes Master. I'm going to do just that. Starting right now."

"Excellent Johnny, I wish you well." He hung up.

Damn it! My new pants!

There are a number of things a Porsche is good at. Attracting hot chicks is one. Getting you somewhere fast is another.

I banged on the door of *Carlyles' Sartorial Emporium* and the 'Sorry we're Closed' sign wobbled beneath the impact of my fists. Closed? I felt like I'd been punched in the stomach, and I doubled-up, hands on my knees. Gone, too late to be the beautiful peacock the

Master had insisted on. I screwed up my eyes as the disappointment grew into sorrow. It wasn't like I could just come back tomorrow.

A key turned in a lock and the door opened.

I raised my head and saw Cyril Sneer's haughty expression.

"I had just finished clearing up and was about to leave. Would you like your trousers now, sir?"

"Cyril... I...I'm sorry I called you Cyril. That was mean of me and unwarranted. What's your name?"

"Cecil, sir."

Oh. Maybe not that mean after all.

"Okay Cecil, can I be a tiny bit more of a burden on your generous nature and have you pick out some appropriate shoes and a shirt for me?"

He closed his eyes and inclined his head.

"Of course, sir. We never turn away a repeat customer. Right this way."

He selected a pair of very simple black shoes and presented them to me as I swapped my jeans for the suit pants.

"Are they just a bit too stuffy?"

"On the contrary. They are elegant and becoming a gentleman."

Eight hundred bucks of hand stitched gentleman. I shrugged.

I picked out a flame red silk shirt with strong collars, explaining the Master's philosophy to Cecil.

"I think you'll find, sir, that there is an inherent contradiction between the words 'gentleman' and 'peacock'."

The compromise was labeled Versace, very bright and it cost more than the shoes.

"I take it that I am unlikely to be able to persuade you of the merits of a fine tie, sir?"

I held up my palms and backed away from him. "I have never worn a tie in my life, and I intend to die that way."

"I suspected as much, sir. Then perhaps the dash of a pocket square? It can add a certain panache to an outfit, when correctly folded."

"A what now?" He handed me a piece of silk that complimented the Versace. "Oh, a handkerchief."

Cecil frowned and pinched the brow of his nose. "Pocket square, sir."

"Handkerchief."

"Pocket—oh never mind. There is, I suppose, a limit to how far one can civilize an American."

Some of the finer details like cufflinks I left to his greater experience, and at the cash register Cecil threw in a pair of socks, with his compliments.

The credit card I had no intention of ever repaying took another heavyweight body blow. I tweaked my cuffs until the links glinted beneath. I was looking sharp and I knew it.

Chapter 10: The Urban Sophisticate

7:01 pm

I didn't see too many sunsets in a city with skyscrapers this tall, and evening had rolled in by the time I left Cecil's store. I sat in the car, my phone in my hand, trying to work out where to go next.

The Master said I had to lift my game. Push myself to loftier goals. I thumbed through my contacts until I got to Kirsten. Wow. She was damned hot. Madison, eep! I blushed and swiped onto the cop girl. Now that the terror of that whole encounter was behind me I was able to rate her calmly. Very hot. The link to her FriendBook page said she was called Victoria. No last names but looking through the photos she had posted I could see why she kept a bit of anonymity.

"There you are! I've been looking all over for you!"

I looked up and a tall woman in a long green strapless dress swept down the steps of *L'Ermitage de Parisienne*, pointing a small clutch purse at me.

"The consommé was ghastly and you're four minutes late."

She was very tall, beautiful but with a stern tightness around her eyes and the corners of her mouth had a tiny downward slant. Her hair was pinned back at the sides and twisted around a fan at the back, flattering the large pink diamonds in her earrings. She tapped three times on the top of my car door. Tap, tap, tap of immaculate red nails the same color as the Porsche.

"Well?" She stared at me, unblinking, and I felt like I was about to tell her I hadn't done my homework.

"Um, what?"

"Move over, idiot. I'm driving." She opened the door and I managed to clamber sideways without turning my back on her, negotiating the stick shift as it threatened to do to me what The Beast had failed to a couple of hours earlier.

She slammed the door shut and glared at me. "I'm not paying for those four minutes. Not at your rates."

"Em, wha—" was all I managed as she did something complicated with the pedals, twisted the steering wheel and yanked up on the hand brake at the same time. The Porsche screamed as it spun in the road, smoke billowing out from under the rear arches and the acrid stink of burning rubber in the air. The handbrake went down, my head snapped back as I was crushed into the passenger seat. She gunned for second gear and we were flung into the street.

I grabbed for the safety belt as soon as I could force my white knuckled grip from the edges of the seat. I glanced at her and she was smiling with bared teeth as we wove around the traffic like a drunken red bullet.

"Maybe it would be safer if you slowed down a bit?"

She rounded on me, lip raised in a snarl. "I don't do safe."

"Okay," seemed the quickest way to get her attention off me and back on the road.

The roller coaster trip probably only took about twenty minutes, but each minute was filled with a series of heart-stopping terrors and choked cries from me of "Watch out!", "Wait for the—", and "I think that light was red..." By the time we stopped outside a swanky apartment in the most expensive street in the city I wore a vacant, thousand yard stare, unable to do any more than mumble incoherently to myself.

She threw my keys to an elderly man in a brass-buttoned grey greatcoat with maroon lapels. His peaked hat had a trim of gold braid.

"Good evening, ma'am. You're looking resplendent tonight."

Resplendent? I'm twenty-four years old and I swear I have never uttered that word. I mouthed it silently.

"Thank you, Carmichael," she said.

She hitched her dress up an inch with the hand that held the clutch purse and flowed through the door that Carmichael held open for her.

"Hi," I said as I walked past and he tilted his hat to me.

The mirrored elevator was too hot and my neck prickled. She stared at me, still not blinking, and I felt dampness starting to form at the base of my spine.

"You better be worth it," she said, the faintest trace of warmth in her voice for the first time. A twitch of a smile one corner of her mouth, then it was gone.

The elevator pinged at the penthouse floor and the doors whispered open. The short hallway led only to one door. She sashayed to it, reaching into her clutch. Some keys jingled and she went inside. Feeling oddly voyeuristic, I followed her.

The condo was an homage to shades of white, more lifeless and sterile than the hospital in which today's journey had begun. As she moved through it lights came on automatically, muted with a hint of blue. The entrance hall was paved in a pale marble and her hammer-on-nail heel taps took her across the hall, down a couple of white steps and into a sunken living area. The whole side of the room was glass, with a balcony beyond and the view encompassed half the city, the last glow of orange in the distance as purples melted to black above.

She settled on a white leather armchair, her back straight, arms spread wide across the backrest and crossed her leg at the knee. The elevated foot tapped silently in the air. I'd been in less stressful job interviews and breathed shallowly, from my belly.

"What's your name, or working name, whatever?" Her roving stare settled on my shoes and she gave the faintest nod. I thanked Cecil for my small reprieve.

"Um... Johnny. Hi." Hoping she wouldn't notice I pressed my palms to my thighs, trying to dry them.

She noticed, and smiled on one side of her face. "Do you know who I am?"

Was I supposed to? She was beautiful enough to be an actress but I couldn't quite place her.

"I'm Bianca Vandersnatch."

My eyes widened. "Of the diamond co—"

"My diamond company, yes. You will, of course, be discrete in our dealings."

"Of course..." I mumbled.

"Because if you decide a quick buck for some paparazzi sensation is worth your time, well..." She snapped her fingers. "I'll have you killed."

I was starting to feel very cold; measuring the distance back to the door, a splinter of light showing it was still ajar. If I just ran, sprinted as fast as I could, would I make it to the lift before she caught me? What the hell was I thinking? She looks like a socialite but... is she some kind of serial killer?

"Look..." I cleared my throat twice and she crooked up that side of her mouth again as my voice trembled. "I think there's been some kind of mistake—"

"No mistake. You're my gigolo. Not bad looking, though I'd have preferred someone taller. No matter, we're here now so you'll have to do. Drink?"

I definitely needed a drink. "Sure. Great! Thanks."

She trailed her arm from the backrest and pointed past me. My head swiveled and I saw the drinks cabinet, stacked with as many bottles and mixers as a public bar. Oh sweet baby Jesus. She thinks I'm a gigolo and I can make her cocktails. I can't make cocktails!

"Scotch rocks. Glenmorangie, if I have any left. Oh and put some music on. I don't care what."

Phew.

I took stiff steps there and slid open the glass. She had cut crystal tumblers, and after a few moments searching I poured out two stiff measures. A bit more rooting around and I found a fridge installed in the bottom of the cabinet and plopped a couple of cubes in each glass with the silver tongs that I found there. Why was I still playing along?

Her music collection was all classical. Orchestral, chamber music, opera. Not actually knowing any of the pieces, I chose some Mozart at random. I couldn't go wrong with Mozart, could I?

Mustering what little courage I had that wasn't squeaking for me to run and hide, I walked back to her, trying to manage what I hoped came across as a casual swagger. The violins began with breathless clarity from speakers hidden somewhere about the room.

"Why are you limping?"

I straightened up. "Nothing. Just a twinge. It's gone now."

She brushed her fingers against mine as she took the tumbler. "Thank you, Johnny."

I wanted to clear my throat again but was starting to feel like an idiot. Surely this was exactly the sort of thing the Master was talking about? I needed to up my game. I took half the whiskey in one gulp then coughed for real as the stuff burned my throat.

Bianca laughed quietly once. "You're very tense, Johnny. You should just relax; it will be more fun for both of us that way. Why don't we start off with a strip tease?"

Her crooked smile had now dimpled her cheek. I took in the line down the side of her neck, across her collarbone, and down the valley that disappeared into the green of her dress. With the little whiskey glow warming my chest, calming my nerves, I could finally start to appreciate her. Her sheer, faultless skin and the sharp edge of her jaw made her seem like a perfect statue in a museum. With each sip of her whiskey the tightness in her lips lessened and their color broke the illusion, making her almost human and attainably desirable.

I managed a chuckle. "Strip tease? Well, yeah, that would be awesome."

I settled in the chair opposite her, waiting for her to begin. She arched an eyebrow.

"Not me, darling. You're the one getting paid to get me off, remember?"

"Oh right. Of course, Sorry, my bad." I finished the rest of the whiskey and set the glass down. It rattled as I released it.

My hands shook as I stood up. Bianca tilted her head slightly as she regarded me, and I let the whisky do to me what it does best. I began to move my hips and my fingers played with the fastened button on the front of my jacket.

"Da, da, da..." I sung not particularly tunefully, and popped the set the candle on the cabinet beside me and rifled through the drawer again.

She descended on me, holding a long strip of red silk and she wrapped it around my head and tied it so that my eyes were covered. Despite the goosebumps covering my skin I felt myself start to sweat, a clammy chill starting at the base of my spine and crawling in prickly steps around my torso.

"Ouch!" What I assumed was another dribble of hot wax fell on my cock and I felt it twitching at the bizarre sensation.

"Does that feel good, slave?" She paused, then in *sotto voce* said, "You can answer that."

"Erm, no, ah, Mistress Pain. It hurts."

"Does the slave wish me to stop?"

"Yes please!"

I yelped as more wax scalded my poor penis. Despite the discomfort I felt the heat causing me to swell and I began to rise up like a flagpole.

"You will address me as Mistress Pain at all times!"

"Yes please Mistress Pain!"

A phone rang; the default manufacturer's tune selection.

"Is that yours or mine?" Madison was back.

"Mine's in my jacket," I said tensing myself for a lash that never came, and the ringing continued.

I heard a rustle as she pulled my phone out and squeaked her excitement.

button, spreading the jacket from the lapels. I shuffled my feet, turning slowly, then looked over my shoulder at her, pulling the jacket down a bit and moving it from side to side as I wriggled.

Bianca laughed, the ice chinking in her tumbler as she leaned forward, resting her elbows on her knees.

"Have you never danced for a woman before?"

"Erm... I dance in front of the TV... well no, not in front of a woman..."

"Your moves are intriguing—entertaining maybe—but not sexy. Definitely not sexy. How long have you been an escort for?"

I stopped my undulations. "To be honest? Not long. Not long at all actually."

Bianca put her glass down. "Push your chair nearer to mine. We'll try something else."

She left the room and returned with a small packet in her hands, watching me rearrange the furniture. Our armchairs were separated only by a low circular glass table. She opened the packet and laid a deck of cards on the table.

"Do you play poker, darling?"

"No," I admitted. I wasn't getting very far with this charade and I suspected she could see right through me.

"Then I'll teach you as we play. A simplified game for a beginner."

Bianca riffled the pack and dealt us each five cards. She smiled as she put down the rest of the pack then she picked up her cards, fanning them out, took a quick glance then laid them face down on the table.

"Look at your cards. You can throw away up to three and you'll get fresh ones from the pack, but remember; that will be your final hand."

I fanned mine out like she had done and scanned them. "How do I know what is good?"

"It's quite simple. Two pairs is better than one and three of a kind better than that. Three is beaten by a straight, when all the numbers are in a row, and that loses to a flush, when they are all the same suite. Better than that is a full house, when you hold three and a pair. You think you've got that?"

I seesawed my hand. "Kind of..."

"Don't worry, darling. I won't cheat you. Now, how many cards do you want?"

I put three on the table and she dealt me replacements. As I picked them up and fanned them again she brushed her top card toward the deck and drew a single fresh card from the pack. Bianca turned a corner up to check, then placed it face down on top of her others.

"Now what?" I said.

"Now we see who has the best hand. Put your down so I can see them."

I did, and she turned hers over, spreading them out in a line.

"You lose. Don't worry it's mostly luck. Mostly. I'm sure you'll get lucky... sometime. Now, lose something."

I slung my jacket over the back of the chair, turning back as she dealt more cards. I had three fives. I dropped the two others, but the cards that came back were not much better. We laid our cards on the table.

Bianca pouted. "Bah! A terrible hand. You win, darling." She turned her head as she unhooked her earrings, laying the pink glittering things next to her cards.

"Jewelry counts? I thought we had to take off clothes?"

"It's just a game. Besides, you have so much more to lose than I do, don't you?" She traced a finger down her bare throat, across the slope of her breast and stopped at the top of her dress.

I had an involuntary deep breath when she touched herself and she betrayed a small smile seeing me do it.

"Not yet, darling. You'll have to learn to play better."

More cards were dealt and my shirt joined my jacket. The next hand, the same thing happened.

"If your earrings counted, then does my belt count too?"

She pursed her lips. "Belt and shoes then. And be a darling and open some champagne, would you? There should be a couple of Krugs in the chiller."

I padded in my socks back to the drinks cabinet and wrestled with the cork, squeaking as the thing popped through my fingers then rushing to get the frothing flow into tall flutes with stems so slender I worried that my pincer grip would shatter them.

"*A votre santé!* We're having fun already, aren't we?"

I was shirtless in front of one of the richest women in the country, who was incredibly hot, and I was entertaining the high likelihood that we'd be having sex soon.

"Absolutely." We clinked glasses and drank, the fine froth unlike anything I'd tasted before. Which admittedly only included beer, but this merited a crossing off somewhere.

She dealt more cards; I chewed on my lip as I tried to work out which ones to drop.

"It's meant to be a fast game. Don't make it boring."

I eventually exchanged two, immediately regretted it when I saw what I got back, sighed and pulled off my socks.

"Is that fair? I don't have any socks." She wiggled perfectly pedicured and painted toes from her silver strappy high heels.

I took a deep breath and dropped by pants. At least the champagne had got me to a golden place where I didn't feel the slightest bit embarrassed anymore.

"Darling! Is that what I think it is?"

I could get used to this kind of reception. Pity it was only for a few more hours. I sat back down again and tapped the table.

"You'll need to keep winning to find out."

Bianca giggled, the first girlish gesture I'd seen from her, then she dealt the next hand.

Ooo—three tens. And the ace of hearts.

"You look a bit flushed. Is it too hot in here for you?" Bianca watched me closely.

"Just the champagne, which is excellent I might add. More?"

"Please." Bianca held out her flute and I topped it off. She frowned at her cards then laid them flat as usual.

I placed a single card down for replacement.

"Only one, darling?"

I tried to shrug calmly but I think it looked more like a twitch. I picked up the replacement. Ace of spades. I placed my cards on the table as Bianca swapped two of hers.

"Ready?" My hand hovered over my cards.

"I'm always ready," said Bianca.

I turned mine over and jumped up. "Woo-hoo! Three and a pair! Full house wasn't that?"

She finished her champagne and put down her glass, rising smoothly like a green flag, then turning her back to me. She didn't even turn her cards over.

"Help me with the catch at the top, darling. I can't reach it myself."

I smelled her perfume as I came close, acutely aware that I was breathing on her neck. She was taller than me in her suicide heels. My fingers twitched as I tried to work the catch lose, my knuckles pressing against her flesh for the first time, what had seemed like marble was warm and soft and yielding. The catch came lose and the zip was beneath.

"Carry on, darling. It's still strip poker whether I take my clothes off or you do it." Her voice was much lower and softer, almost a husky breath.

The dress unzipped past the waist, parting to reveal the clasp of a black bra, then lower beneath the shadowed dell at the base of her spine, a lacy stripe of the top of her panties. I stepped back, realizing that my hands had stopped trembling and my breathing had accelerated. Bianca turned around, batting her eyelashes as she glanced coyly at me. Her arm was across her breasts, holding the dress up and when I met her gaze she let go, the cloth falling like green petals around her ankles.

Those ancient statues had nothing on the tight, curving lines that seemed to spiral down her legs, toes pointed in those heels so high I couldn't see how she had driven so aggressively in them. Bianca stroked back an invisible stray strand at her temple, hips shifting slightly as she did so and I throbbed with desire for her.

"Do you want to play another hand, darling?"

The time for games was over; my lust brought me a new confidence. She wasn't challenging me anymore, she was welcoming me.

"No," I said, my voice thick and strange to my ears. "Let's do something else."

"Follow me," she said, hooking a finger at me then sailing away, those impossibly long legs shifting in figure-eights, a model moving down a catwalk. Up the stairs, and I followed her, entranced by her willowy motions.

"Wait here," she said, and entered the kitchen. The lights flicked into life but she tapped a pad by the door and they faded to a faint hue. Through the doorway I saw that the white marble now changed into black granite, polished to a mirror surface like speckled obsidian. The matching kitchen units parted for a broad range cooker with aluminum and glass hood above it.

She opened a tall fridge and looked back at me waiting in the doorway. The light from the fridge outlined her in high contrast and I felt sure I could pick out that crease of a smile down one side of her face in the darkened room. Bianca walked back to me holding a glass bowl of fruit and a small white pitcher. She didn't meet my gaze that jumped from place to place on her body, and she drifted past.

"Come," she said, and I followed.

Bianca's bedroom was as lifeless as the living room, white shag carpet and white walls, the scarlet sheets and the colorful Rothko on the wall breaking her tradition. Passion reserved for the bed? I hoped so.

She set the bowl and pitcher on the nightstand and pulled a short bottle from a drawer. This was tossed to me, it smelled of ylang-ylang and was a touch oily around the cap.

"I think we'll start with massage, and to avoid any confusion, that means you do me. Okay, darling?"

"I understand." My voice was alien to me, I'd never spoken to a woman with such surety before, let alone one as divine as her.

"Good. Now, Johnny. You may undress me."

In a movie you would stop time right now. You would come to a tight shot of my face, and you would find me asking myself what the one thing in the world I wanted to do above all others was. This was it.

Bianca turned her back to me again and stood still and silent. I kissed her on the back of her neck, across her shoulders and her head arched back. I ran a finger down the groove of her spin and she pressed back to me almost imperceptibly then I ran my palms across her shoulder blades, down the outsides of her arms and she sighed. I unhooked her bra in one movement and pressed my bare chest against her as it fell to the ground; the hard bulge in my shorts pressing against the yielding softness of her buttocks. I feathered my hands across her breasts, slowing as the tips of her nipples drew across my palms, then across her hard belly, sweeping out to the softening of her hips and I hooked my thumbs over the tops of her panties. She tensed.

"My lady?" I whispered into the side of her neck.

"Yes," she said, a dreamy half-awake mumble.

I put my lips to the loose strands at the base of her hairline and lowered myself, slowly, brushing my lips down her as I descended. I knelt behind her and eased her panties past her hips, kissing the pale globes revealed, then tortured by arousal put the edges of my teeth to them.

She gasped. "Gently, darling. Do it, but gently."

I nibbled my way across them and she leaned over, resting her hands on the bed, presenting her sex to me as her cheeks parted. I put my nose to her, inhaling her musk, feeling my pulse through my whole body, absorbing her. I lightly tongued her lips, then licked down the middle, tasting her own moisture beginning to build and she moaned.

"Yes, darling. That's wonderful."

I closed my eyes, willing myself to control my delirium, took a slow breath and stood.

She looked over her shoulder at me. "What are you doing? Keep going."

"Tantalize," I said, and I knew that across the city the Master had smiled.

I nudged her forward and she fell upon the bed, then crawled fully onto it. Bianca laid out straight, resting her head on her bent arm. I cracked open the bottle of oil and smelt it deeply. The ylang-ylang essential oil was soothing, quelling the unruly emotions that clouded my mind. I poured a little onto my palm, then rubbed them together, warming my hands. She stirred, opening her eyes.

"Hush," I said, and climbed on the bed, knees either side of her hips but not resting on her.

My hands went to her the sides of her neck and I began to knead the taut cords there.

"So tense," I said. "Just relax and let me take care of things."

Bianca just signed and I continued to work her neck, then spread wider and dragged my thumbs across her shoulders.

"Yes... harder. I'm so stiff."

"How did you get so tense? You hit the gym a lot?"

"*Jai alai*, darling. I always play to win."

"Oh... wow." I could totally imagine her destroying guys on court.

She was truly an awesome woman. I felt more than respect for her, I felt admiration and I wanted to please her.

I drove my fingertips in deeper, slow strong movements. I was worried that I'd hurt her, or bruise her, but her soft moans continued as I worked on each upper arm in turn. Not having ever given or received a massage did not appear to be a problem. She liked to be stroked and to be rubbed and to have each tight band of muscle kneaded into relaxed pliancy. I applied more oil as needed and continued my exploration of her anatomy.

After a minute where I had been rubbing her second calf, both hands clasped around her leg with my thumbs rotating on the muscle, she half rolled onto her hip, drawing her knee up and slipping her foot through my fingers. I realized that I hadn't found a single hair or even peachy fuzz anywhere on her body, which magnified the feeling that she was otherworldly, made from an alien substance, unnatural purity. She beckoned me.

"Lovely, darling, I feel divine. Now come to me. I want to see what else you can do."

I shuffled from the bed and removed my shorts, springing free with reliable readiness. I grinned at her, anticipating the reaction.

"Now I see why you turned pro. It would be a travesty to have that reserved for the pleasure of a single woman."

Bianca leaned back on her elbows. Her breasts were large for such a slim, fit woman, and they remained perkily upright, her nipples pointing at my face. My gaze travelled down her flat belly, to the swelling of her bare white mound and the line that disappeared in shadow between her closed legs.

"Are you hungry, Johnny?" The edge of her mouth turned up. The narrowing of her lips that I'd come to associate with her taking control.

I hadn't eaten for hours and on her question my stomach rumbled its reply.

"You do like cream, don't you?"

"Sure, everyone likes cream, don't—"

"Then you may eat off me. The rules are that you can place anything on my body, but may only use your lips and tongue to take the food. Have you seen a cat eat, darling?"

I had and knew this was exactly the sort of thing I should have had on The List from the beginning. I'd been teasing her with my massage, now she was teasing me, dominating me, controlling my access to her, limiting it to a single set of conflicting desires; for food and for her. It wasn't the whisky or the champagne in my system. It was her. She intoxicated me.

I took the small fruit knife and laid wafer slices of peach across her breast, circling her nipple that swelled as goosebumps formed around her areola. She shivered as I made a dotted trail of half grapes that meandered from her ribs, across her belly and stopped and the hill and valley of her hip bones. She had goosebumps stippled across on her thighs as I placed thin slices of mango over the rise of her *mont de Venus*.

"Very pretty, darling, well done. And now, the pitcher?"

I reached for it, knelt beside her on the bed, then let a thin trickle of it pool in the depression between her collar bones and she cooed. The white line snaked its way down to the peaches, circling, then weaving around and between the grapes, then over the mangoes, a tiny waterfall between her legs.

I replaced the pitcher and looked at her. I felt like I'd been transported to an ethereal domain that would melt away if I thought too hard about it.

"Bianca... would you mind if I quickly ran and got my phone?"

"You want to make a call? When I'm like this?" Her brow creased in the middle and her lips went very pale and thin.

"No! I just... I just want to take a photo of you. I never want to forget this moment..."

She chuckled. "I thought I'd lost you for a moment. You want to make a sex tape? Fine. Go on, but hurry up, I'm getting cold here. I need you to warm me up."

I was up and running, skidding across the marble in the hallway, nearly tripping down the stairs. Socks and marble don't mix and I stripped them off. Rifled my jacket, phone in hand, bare feet slapping back up the stairs.

I was breathless as I ran back into the bedroom, panting as I framed her body on the screen. She wagged a cross finger at me.

"No head shots, darling. Give the camera to me. I'll decide what you can keep. Now begin."

I handed her my phone and she turned it on me, panning across her body and the feast that awaited then straight at me as I approached, down to below my waist, a pause, then up to my face. I waved.

The bed creaked as I clambered back on board and I knelt beside her, lowering my head and began to lap at the cream strands across her throat. She sighed.

"Breathe on me, Johnny. I need you to warm me up."

I did as she commanded, heating up her shoulders then returning to the trail that ran down her décolleté and up the slope of her breast. I ate carefully, taking each piece of peach between my teeth, chewing it, swallowing it then licking up the juice that remained on her skin. I sucked the cream from her nipple and she arched herself with a moan. The last of the sweet milk gone I held her lightly between my teeth, she let out a soft cry and I released her, following the white trail lower.

The dance down her belly, pausing as I chewed each half grape, had her twisting her hips, in a ragged slow dance. By the time I hovered over her mound, smelling the sweet of the mangoes, she had dropped my phone and clawed the red bed sheets between twitching fingers, pushing up, trying to reach me.

My breathing was heavy now and as she pulsed closer to my lips I slid my hands under her, grasping her cheeks that flexed and bucked, and holding her steady I began to eat the mango slices. By the time I'd finished the last slice, and the last of the sticky juice on her bare mound she exhaled in short gasping pants. My tongue flicked her button, she hissed, and I moved lower, lapping at the cream that had trickled between her labia.

Bianca's legs locked around me, the straps of her heels scratching my back, pulling me harder against her sex, rocking her hips as I performed on her. Her fists tightened on the twisted sheets and she ground herself against me as my mouth covered the most sensitive part of her. Suddenly she released the sheets, half rising from the bed, grabbed my head and cried out, again and again, each one less pained and softer than the last until she released me and sank back down onto the sheets.

She reached for me with one hand, her other slowly stroking herself across her breast and belly. I took her hand and her grip was softer and more yielding than anything she had done before. Had I melted the ice princess? I lay next to her and she guided me onto my back and nuzzled against my chest.

Bianca's breathing slowed to normal and just when I thought she might be falling asleep she turned her head and looked at me, her expression soft and with a natural smile that lacked all the predator's leer that I'd seen from her until then.

"Almost worth your entire fee, darling."

"Bianca, I—"

"Hush, there, there." She raised herself on one elbow, her breast pressing against me. "I haven't finished with you yet."

"What do you want me to do?"

121

"Maybe it is my turn, darling."

She rustled in the nightstand and returned with a foil wrapper. Sitting astride my thighs she unrolled the silicone skin, raised up her hips, brushing me between her nether lips.

Bianca teased me with quarter-inch penetrations before pulling back. I was starting to raise my hips just like I'd made her do, and I think that was probably her intent.

"How long do you think you can last, Johnny?" She circled her hips and I slipped a bit further inside her.

"Not long, to be honest." Looking up at her sculptured from, my hands gently tugging on her hips, I knew this to be true.

She made a small moue then laughed.

"Very well, enough teasing," she said then I penetrated her fully and I groaned loudly.

Bianca leaned forward, gripping me by the shoulders, holding me down as she gyrated. Maybe it was my light-headedness but she felt stronger than me, I guess I'm not exactly Superman after all. I couldn't stroke into her, she controlled the rhythm. She humped me until I started to get close, then clamped hard against me, denying me release. Then she would grind and gyrate, heating me up before giving me penetrative stokes, building me up then freezing again. She watched me intently as my head thrashed from side to side, eyes rolling back and then screwing tight with frustration.

"Bianca, please..."

"Tell me, beg me..."

"Please!"

She kissed me savagely, crazed and I tasted blood on my lip, then she rode me hard and deep, again and again until I shook, staring up at her marble perfection. A sacrifice at the goddess's altar. I think she knew how I felt at that moment for she smiled benignly at me; a higher being's gentleness for a poor creature coming as close as they ever will to majesty.

I lay in a trance and when my eyes shut she slipped off me, took a cigarillo from a silver case by the bed and lit it. Propped up by her pillow she watched me and the heavy smoke took what little slumber I had. I looked at her, brazenly naked, she hadn't even drawn the sheets around her, but had demurely crossed her high-heeled feet at her ankles.

"That was wonderfully intense lovemaking, darling. I don't think I've felt that close to anyone for years. Oh! Literally years. Tell me, are you truly an escort? With such passion?"

What would she do if I told her the truth? That it was all an accident, even a wonderful scary and sexy accident like this. She'd already warned me that she'd have me killed if I betrayed her. I'd seen sides to her that made me think that it was true. Besides, it wasn't as if I had much a future in any case.

"Maybe, Bianca, it is you. You are a very special woman."

She let the smoke roll out of her mouth and the hard glint returned to her eyes, "As I thought. It wasn't real passion. You're smooth, I'll give you that."

"Bianca, I—"

"Never mind, I'm fine. I'm not some little girl whose feelings you're going to hurt."

The moment was gone and her armor of ice once again covered her soul. She ground out the half smoked cigarillo and got up.

"Time for a shower then we're going out," she said.

"Out? Where?"

"I promised to go to a party tonight and I can't walk in alone or there will be completely the wrong kind of gossip. A deliciously naughty little boy like you on my arm will create exactly the right kind of gossip. Besides you'll enjoy it. All the right people will be there."

I hesitated; this was my last night on earth. Was that where I wanted to be?

Bianca patted me on the chest. "Don't worry, darling. I won't monopolize you. We'll arrive, smile for the press, say hello to a few people then you can slip from my arm and do whatever your fancy takes you."

"Okay, that sounds fine. Great I mean."

She slipped off the bed and started to walk toward the door the silvery straps of her heels looking like the crests of ripples in a harbor by moonlight. "I'll leave the water running for you, darling. I'll only be a few minutes rinsing the last of this cream off."

I hadn't noticed that I'd left any cream on her and a pang of disappointment coursed through me. I heard the gush then the hiss of the shower starting, and picking up my phone I followed her. I

124

replayed the video, the sound muted. OMG, she was hysterically hot. I couldn't believe that the male talent in the movie was me. I skipped forward, to almost the end and saw the slant-angled shot, half obscured by a crumple in the sheets, of her snuggling against me. That side of her was locked inside somewhere. I nearly got it out but it slipped through my fingers.

I sighed, knowing that this was one question where I'd never find out the answer.

I was not surprised by the chrome and alabaster walk-in shower room. Bianca walked past me, toweling her hair as I stepped under the hot stream. Her potions and lotions all smelled suspiciously girlie to me, but I embraced my inner peacock and lathered up.

Bianca sat with her back to me, doing her makeup and didn't speak as I collected my shorts. I dressed in the living room, spread The List on the table, smiled at my childish naiveté whilst adding an entry and striking it through in one go.

~~Number 31: Eat food off a beautiful woman's body~~

But there was also an original one that could now be dealt with:

~~Number 18: Make a sex tape~~

Chuckling at my puerile lack of imagination, I noticed her poker hand still lying face down on the table. I kept looking at them and wondering as I did up my cuff links, then I turned them over.

Huh.

I was just slipping my jacket back on and checking the contents of my pockets when Bianca strode in. She paused at the top of the stairs and, like they say in the movies, my jaw hit the floor. She'd swept her hair back into the same fan, but her evening dress was a silver embroidered black sash that went from shoulder to hip, covering her breasts and leaving almost everything else exposed. She looked more naked than when she'd been lying on the bed. The lower half of the dress, in the palest pink embroidered with black, trailed on the floor but had been slashed away to the hip on one side so that with each step you had a flash of the entire length of her naked leg then the cloth fluttered and it was snatched away from you. Her heels were even taller than before, stack-soled and iridescing like mercury.

"Bianca..."

She nodded, towering imperiously over me, and held out her hand, a yellow twinkle from the diamond like a crystal acorn on her ring.

"You look incredible..."

Her smile was very small and she nodded. "Thank you, darling."

"Bianca, before we go I need to ask you one thing."

I pointed at her turned over cards on the table. "What do you call having a perfect series of all diamonds?"

"It's called a straight flush, didn't I tell you that?"

"Maybe, I don't remember. Does it beat my full house?"

"Why, yes it does."

"So why did you throw the game? I thought you said you always play to win."

"That depends on the game I'm playing, the way I see it, I won. You were ghastly and nervous when you got here, and I had to do something about that. When you thought you'd beaten me you relaxed completely, you felt more equal to me and I got what I deserved."

Bianca took a roll of bills from a fist-sized black clutch purse and inserted it in my top pocket. "You were worth every cent, I'd say."

"Oh," I said. "Oh!" My cheeks grew hot. She was complimenting me!

"Ah, that proves it. You were never my real escort, were you? I must have terrified the life out of you, you poor thing! Just jumping into your car and driving you here. Well, all things considered your poise was admirable. Hand me your phone."

She took it from me, typed for a moment then handed it back.

"Now, darling," she said. "You may take me to the ball."

Chapter 11: Genes of Sweden; I Salute You.

8:28 pm

I wasn't feeling any braver with Bianca at the wheel so I settled for just covering my eyes with one hand and clutching the seat belt over my chest with the other. We screeched to a halt and I chanced a peek. The sidewalk was a blinding mess of strobing lamps. A bellboy opened the driver's door and held it as Bianca swung her crossed ankles out of the car and stood elegantly, one hand at her hip, the other cocked behind her head.

The random lamps all scorched together and from behind them cries of, "Bianca, Bianca..." and "This way Ms. Vandersnatch!" I shut the door and moved around the back, standing a few paces away from her. Bianca had a wide-mouthed toothy smile on as she preened for the reporters. She tossed her head to call me over and I dutifully approached, put my arm around her waist and pulled her close to me.

The press pack erupted again and microphones were thrust at us as comments were demanded by Jenny Unpronounceable from Station

X and Gerry Generic from **KFCNFL** News.

Bianca hissed at me. "Smile, darling. You're dating a beautiful billionaire; you ought to look ecstatic about it!"

I beamed my biggest smile like an actor in a toothpaste commercial that wanted to share my unbridled joy with the world. Bianca swooned against my shoulder, then tightening her grip on my hand she led me through the throng. Past burly black-suited men in sunglasses who kept the living tide of press-passes back from us. Up the richly carpeted stairs, past marbled colonnades and through high oak doors into a reception hall.

The hall was broadly oval, with two balustraded staircases curving around the walls on each side to join at a small balcony above. The ceiling soared above us, painted in a classical style, cherubs frolicking with angels amongst the clouds. Behind the balcony was an opening to another room and I could see the tips of sparkling chandeliers beyond. Piano music was playing, dignified and discrete, something I'd have found in Bianca's collection no doubt.

There was little room to move in the reception hall and the guests made their excuses each time they had to shuffle closer. Two white-jacketed gentlemen appeared at the balcony, separating they swept down each of the stairways and stopped with a white-gloved hand on each of the red ropes that bared the bottom of the staircases. They turned to look up the stairs, waited as the hubbub of the crowd had diminished to whispers and murmur, and a gong rang brightly and clearly.

The red ropes drew aside and in pairs the guests began to ascend the staircases.

Bianca clicked her tongue. "I can't believe I have to wait like everyone else. I swear he is doing it to tease me. The little shit."

"Bianca!" I couldn't imagine what could had put a dent into her 24 karat ego, so I just patted her hand that was draped through the crook of my arm.

She puffed away an imaginary lock of hair, closed her eyes and breathed deeply. "I'm sorry, Johnny. In normal situation I'm treated as respectfully as I deserve, but he—ooo! He always acts so natural, as if he doesn't know what I'm talking about, but he still does it. Just because he's a trillionaire. Little shit."

I was going to ask who she was talking about but we moved closer to the base of the stairs and I didn't want to rile her further so her hand got another reassuring pat and I left it at that.

At the top of the stairs fluttered a gaggle of plain girls with too much makeup on. They fussed over each guest who attained the summit, selecting for each of them a mask. Some were simple black figure eights, others decorated with sequins, or rhinestones, or feathers. I received a dark oval one with a peak for the bridge of my nose and put it on hoping I looked a bit like a dashing Zorro.

Bianca's mood had not improved as we neared the party. She stamped her foot and waved the mask girls away from her.

"I will not! Get those dreadful things away from me. Everyone knows who I am, mask or no mask. The whole thing is ridiculous. I'm truly sorry I came to his childish party, even if it is his birthday."

The girls with the masks flushed, glancing to each other then back to Bianca.

"But ma'am! We were told *everyone*—"

"Out of my way! Johnny? Come on!"

Bianca pulled me past the girls as I mumbled my apologies to them.

"Ooo!" She ground her teeth, then slowing our progress she came to a halt and took a deep breath. She smiled at me.

"I suppose you do look a bit dashing in that mask."

I knew it!

She took my crooked arm again and resumed her slow flowing steps. Various people smiled and greeted Bianca as we moved through the crowd, raised their glasses and received a tilt of her head. We stopped in front of an elderly couple, the man bearded and with medals pinned to the breast of his suit, the woman wearing jewels to rival Bianca's.

"Count Otto, so wonderful to see you again. Agatha, it's been far too long." Bianca allowed the count to raise her hand and brush his moustache across her fingers.

"You must excuse me, we'll speak again later. I need to pay my respects to our host."

A gentle tug on my arm and Bianca moved us on. I noticed people looking at me then whispering to their partners as we passed. The good kind of gossip I assume. More rooms led off the main party hall and Bianca craned her neck through the door of each in turn, scanning the people inside, then moving on. Each side room had different types of entertainment laid out. One had a roulette table, another had an elevated platform with a dancing girl wearing little more than the snake twined around her body. We reached a darkened one with lights that twirled in time to the pumping dance music, smoke twisting around people's feet as they grooved together.

"There he is. Follow my lead, darling. Let's see if we can't make that little shit squirm a bit."

Leaning casually with his back to the DJ booth, framed by the speakers, was a tall blond guy, slim but broad shouldered. He wore a black evening suit and his bow tie was loose, hanging down the white ruffles of his dress shirt.

"Darling!" Bianca pulled us toward him, holding her other hand out to him.

He grimaced momentarily then smiled, straightening up and placed his martini glass on the ledge behind him.

"Bianca," he said, his voice raised to be heard above the music, and kissed her hand. "So glad you could make it. I wasn't sure if you'd turn up."

"I wouldn't have missed it for the world, you know that, darling."

He looked at me and held his hand out to shake. "Who's your friend?"

I grinned and pushed the mask up to my forehead. "Hello Marcus, it's been a long time."

"Johnny? Johnny!"

We shook hands then Marcus said, "Ah hell. Come here, champ!" He hugged me, a bit too hard. Marcus had always been taller and stronger than me.

"So what have you been up to? How do you two know each other?"

Bianca hugged my arm, resting her head on my shoulder.

"He is really the most delicious gigolo, darling. I didn't know you two were friends?" She enunciated *gi-ga-lo* very clearly and precisely over the bass throbbing around us.

Marcus spluttered. "Gigolo? Johnny? What? Oh yes, we went to school together. Gigolo? Seriously?"

"It's a long story," I said.

He raised an eyebrow, searched my face, then glanced at my groin. "It's just that, well, you know, your—"

"Totally the opposite problem now. Well, not a problem at all anymore. Kind of an asset."

"Oh... Oh! Right, I see..." He trailed off, darting glances around the room.

Bianca was smiling at him with her one slashed cheek lopsided leer. "Oh dear me, how rude. I didn't mean to make you uncomfortable. I'll leave you boys alone to catch up."

She kissed me on the cheek and patted my bum. "Enjoy the rest of your evening, Johnny. Toodle-oo."

Marcus watched her leave. "Wow. So you and Bianca..."

"Oh, no, not really. Just for the last couple of hours. We hadn't met before," I said.

He blinked at me, then he retrieved his Martini and drained it.

"I think I need another drink. What about you, champ?"

"Sure, Marcus. I'll have what you're having."

He raised his hand and a somberly dressed man in a blue suit, who I hadn't noticed but had been standing a few paces away watching us, trotted over. Marcus spoke to him, the words lost in the music. The man lifted his lapel and spoke into a microphone fixed there, then he pressed a finger to his ear.

"On their way, Mr. Goldenrod." He trotted back to his position a short distance away, clasped his hands behind his back and remained facing us with an unfocused gaze.

"So what have you been up to, Johnny? We kind of lost touch, didn't we? I assume you, well I guess you already know what I'd been up to?"

I drew out my Aphone, held it up and he laughed; we both laughed.

"I'm proud of you Marcus, really," I said. "Every time I use it I remember my best friend. We were a hell of a team, weren't we?"

"We sure were, champ," said Marcus.

"Say," I said. "Do still see Gwen around?"

Marcus glanced past me, undid the second button on his shirt. His brow had a sheen on it. Our drinks arrived on a tray, by the time I'd swirled my olive and taken a sip he'd finished his and had an ice cube up against his temples.

"Phew, it's getting hot in here, isn't it? Have you checked out any of the other rooms? There got to be some crazy shit going on in some of them. Some real party animals here tonight, you know, once the stuffies and coffin-dodgers go home."

"That sounds awesome Marcus. I'm kind of on a roll today, you know, making the most out of every day?"

"That's the spirit, Johnny! Live everyday as if it was your last, that sort of thing?"

"Yes. Exactly that sort of thing. And I wondered, will Gwen be here tonight? Is she around?"

He put his arm around my shoulders, gave me a squeeze, and steered me out the room, glancing back over his shoulder, I suppose at his flunky.

"Nah. It's a shame. She got called away on business at the last minute, had to jump on a plane."

"Oh. I was hoping to talk to her. What kind of work is she in, anyway?"

"She's a teacher at the elementary school here..." Marcus trailed off. We left the club music room and wove our way across the main party hall, heading for a set of closed double doors.

"A teacher? That's great. She was always so good with people. Erm... what kind of business emergency calls an elementary teacher across the country?"

"Erm... whooping cough... or something. A special vaccine, I think."

"She's sick?"

I stopped and Marcus took a step past me then turned back.

"Look, it's no big deal, Johnny. She had a conference or something. I don't really remember. I was on the phone to the head of my Asia-Pacific division, a reporter from the Wall Street Journal and my personal trainer at the same time. All I remember was that she couldn't be here. Now, just forget about her, come and let's have some fun."

The problem was I couldn't just forget about her.

The old Johnny I left behind this morning was created, in part, by her. Her betrayal and my unrequited feelings for her were a model for my life from that point on. Now that I had moved passed that the new Johnny wanted to speak to her one last time before the end.

Two men in black suits with earpieces stepped away from the double doors as Marcus arrived, opening them just enough to slip through.

"Come in, champ. This is the private party room. Only a very special elite get to come in here, and guess what Johnny? You're invited."

The room was darker than the club room, but the music was just as loud. Faster, more driving beats, people cheering and bodies brushing against each other, the first people shuffling their feet and swaying their hips as the dancing started.

Marcus wove his way between the dancers, shaking hands or

kissing cheeks with those he passed. I followed him, ungreeted, unknown, and met him at a glass topped cocktail bar. The barman had left the drink of another customer half poured and leaned toward Marcus, taking his order.

"Johnny! Same again?"

I looked at my half martini and shrugged. "Sure, why not," I said above the music.

The barman turned away. I admired the casual, confident way Marcus leaned on the counter. You didn't need to know who he was, you could see across the room that this was a powerful man, a ruler of worlds. I leaned beside him, trying to capture the pose. It felt a bit awkward.

"So, Marcus. Do you catch up with Gwen often?"

Our drinks arrived; we chinked glasses and sipped them.

"Actually, well the thing of it is; we're engaged."

My heart sank, in fact all of me sank. I sagged against the bar supported only by lifeless legs that started to melt under me. She's gone forever. I tried to bear the vertigo that threatened to swallow me whole, hurting but not wanting Marcus to see. Not wanting to hurt him. At least she was going to a great guy. I tried to think that but it was pale consolation.

"Oh. Congratulations Marcus..."

"Thanks, champ!"

I couldn't think of anything to say and we sat there in as much silence as you can when the room is filled with syncopated beats and the whoops of intoxicated revelers. Why did I keep torturing myself like this? I'd done the same thing through high school. She try to talk to me every now or then, get me alone someplace or hang about after class. I knew what was going to happen, she'd definitely have some horrible thing to say to be, just like she'd told everyone about my micropenis and made my teenage years the hell that they were.

So why did I still want to talk to her, on my last day, when I could be chasing hotties? I finished my drink.

"Marcus, you want another? My round this time."

"Sure, champ. Keep 'em coming."

It took me longer than Marcus to get served. When I turned back to him and he had two tall blondes standing to either side of him; long straight hair that fell just past their shoulders, eyes like blue glass, pink gloss lipstick. They had matching outfits, blue shorts so tiny there was a crease of cheek visible beneath each back pocket and V-necked T-shirts cropped to the top of their ribs and stretched tight over their swimsuit model perfect breasts. Neither wore bras and their nipples poked at the thin cloth.

I did a double-take from one to the other, they actually were twins. One I guess had a very slightly narrower nose, the other slightly higher cheek bones, but if you stood them apart you would have had to try hard to tell which one was which.

"Johnny! Come meet my friends," Marcus said. "These are the Bröstenberg twins. They're Swedish models. Aren't they awesome?"

They giggled then each took me by the shoulder and kissed me on the cheek. They smelled of hot perfume.

"I'm Astrid," said the one on the left. Her accent was very strong. "I'm the oldest."

"I'm Sigrid," said the one on the left. "And I'm the naughtiest!"

They collapsed into a fit of giggles and Marcus grinned at me.

"I have them at my place as *au pairs*!"

"Nice," I said. Lucky, lucky bastard.

Marcus' attention drifted as he took a moment to examine Astrid's cleavage. She pressed her arms together to plump them up. Sigrid took his chin and gently turned his head to her, repeating her sister's performance. He sighed.

"Impossible to say who is best, you're both simply perfect."

Lucky, lucky, lucky bastard.

"Hey Johnny. You know what the best thing about Swedish girls is? They love two things. You know that? Drinking and fucking. Is that right girls?"

They squealed and clapped their hands.

"Marcus," I said. "Do you think two ex-models working as au pairs for an American trillionaire are representative of a whole country's female population?"

"Ah don't be so stiff, Johnny. Or maybe... hey girls, do you prefer him stiff?"

They squealed again and Marcus patted their bottoms, ushering them to me. Astrid and Sigrid draped themselves over me, a good couple of inches taller than me in identical peep-toed high-heel boots.

"Girls, listen up. Johnny is a special friend of mine and I want you to keep him busy in a special way, okay?"

They were already bumping themselves against me in time with the music, urging me to dance. Marcus placed a flat plastic business card in my hand. It had the stylized 'A' that was the Awesome Computers logo, but no other marking.

"That's my key to my private suite. You can get there out the back of the bar and up the stairs. Very private so... be my guest."

"Wow, Marcus. Thanks!"

"No problem champ. Oh, and remember, I know what those two girls are like. Once you get started you won't want to stop. It was great catching up but you don't need to worry about rushing yourself. If we don't catch up again tonight, well that's fine. You won't hurt my feelings. Have fun, Johnny!"

He winked conspiratorially, mouthing *nymphomaniacs* at me. He blew kisses to Astrid and Sigrid then left us.

"We want to dance. Will you? Please?"

Sigrid placed my hand on her bottom as she gyrated in time with the music. Astrid took my other hand and pulled our human caterpillar along until we were in the middle of the dance floor, the best lit part of the room. The Bröstenberg twins started dancing, which mostly involved rubbing their asses against me, bending their knees deeper as they rubbed down the outside of my legs then grinding their way back up. They tossed their heads as they danced, the golden halos of their hair darkening with sweat, stands plastering to their faces, dampening my cheeks and necks as they put their faces near to mine, gazed into my eyes before laughing and spiraling away.

They turned and spun and I'd lost track of which one was who. The twilight of the dancers around us, couples just inches away from the spotlight at the center of the room, girls making eyes at me, batting their lashes, biting their lips. They looked until they caught my eye, then looked away quickly only to furtively sneak another glance. The guys' stares devoured the slim dancing bodies of the Bröstenberg twins, their T-shirts turning translucent with sweat and the glare of the lamps. One dude gave me a thumbs up, applauded me. I laughed. This must be what it feels like to be Marcus Goldenrod, every single day.

I danced like I danced in my house in front of my TV. I guess the girls loved it because they cheered me each time I did a move, clapping their hands, covering their mouths as they laughed, then they would raise their arms, rub against me and we would dance together. People brought us shots; tequila one time, something sweet and green another. Sigrid started doing this thing where she would shimmy in front of me, holding her lips a feather-breadth away from mine and then drag her nipples across my lapels. I could feel my throat constricting as my world became her lips so tantalizingly close. Did I dare move closer, dare kiss her? What if she pulled away and it all ended right there? As my breathing deepened she sighed, breathed me, then spread my shirt so that her soft-hard nubs poking through the damp fabric rubbed my bare chest.

I don't know how long we danced but eventually Sigrid leaned on me, breathing hard. She looked at me closely, twirling a damp strand around her fingertip. Astrid stopped dancing and stood behind her sister, holding her by her hips, resting her head on her sister's shoulder. They stared at me in silence, parted lips and a hint of smiles.

"What?" I said. "Have you had enough dancing?"

"We do everything together," said Sigrid. Her strong accent somewhat slurred now.

"Everything," said Astrid. Her hands slipped up from Sigrid's blue-shorted hips to her bare waist, slid around her belly, then up to encompass her sister's breasts, the T-shirt looking like blurred nylon.

Sigrid's eyelids fluttered closed. The heat had blurred her eye makeup and the mascara was a dark aurora around each. "Johnny, do you want to do us together?"

Thank. You. God.

Had this happened this morning I think I'd probably have simply passed out. A crumpled pile of pallid geek with two intergalactically hot girls looking down at him and scratching their heads. The Johnny of around, say midday, would be stammering and blushing. Now I felt the clarity of anticipation, the deep insistence of my pulse quickening, and the all-consuming desire to be with them, pleasure them and release ourselves in bliss.

I placed a hand at the small of each of their backs and moved them to the exit behind the bar.

"More drinks!" Astrid pulled me to a halt.

"Champagne!" Sigrid waved both arms for the bartender. The sight of her perfectly pert boobies jiggling with only a diaphanous membrane covering them made him get to her faster than he had managed when he was sucking up to Marcus.

"The best champagne," warned Astrid, faking a frown and pointing a wavering finger at me.

"The best champagne," I said to the barman, laying Bianca's roll on the table, spreading out the notes. "Two bottles and chilled glasses, keep the change."

I patted in my pocket and pulled out Marcus' security card. "Oh, I'm going to the private suite. Could someone bring it all up?"

"Right away, Mr. ..." He paused.

"Johnson."

Yes, Mr. Johnson, right away."

I swept the girls along, round the bar and out back, then up echoing white stairs, the muffled pounding of the music fading until all we could hear was its distant pulse.

The stairs carried on up, but at the first flight landing there was a door, Awesome Computers logo on it, and a black security panel on the wall to the side of the door knob. I presented the card, a red light pulsed and the door clicked and cracked open an inch.

The Bröstenberg twins bundled past me and the lights in the room came on.

A husky woman's voice said, "Welcome, Marcus. Would you like music?"

The girls threw themselves on a huge bed in the center of the room, black satin sheets crinkling beneath them.

"Yes," I said, looking around the room and not seeing anyone else there. There was a drinks cabinet, two long brown leather sofas, a door ajar to a tiled bathroom and a glass front to the outside wall. Through its black mirror I could dimly see the lights of city buildings, the snaking lanes of car lights, white streams on one side, red on the other.

Barry White started his melodious rumbling and I saw for the first time a panel display mounted in the wall. The face of a young woman with slicked back hair and only the faintest hints of makeup on her eyes. Her gaze followed me as I walked toward the screen.

She frowned. "You're not Marcus. Please hold."

There was a ringing and a black box appeared in the bottom right of the screen. The ringing stopped and Marcus' face appeared, there was muffled dance music playing, barely audible over Barry's deep crooning and the squealing of the girls on the bed who were rolling over themselves and tickling each other.

"Marcus, there is someone in your room and I don't think it is you. He is not on the employee database either."

Marcus chuckled. "Hey Johnny, are you there, champ?"

"Hey Marcus, who is—"

"This is C.O.C.O., Johnny. My Computer Operated Concierge Officer. Pretty neat, huh? Better than any executive assistant I've had, she's never sick and never takes personal days. Plus, and here is the best bit, no sexual harassment suits if I ask her to find me some porn!"

"Oh, great I guess. I—"

"Coco. Make a database entry. Label: Johnny Johnson. Give him full clearance up to Director. Okay?"

"Yes Marcus." She blinked. "I've done that, Marcus. Will there be anything else?"

"No that's fine. He may be in there for some time. Make sure he isn't disturbed." He winked and his picture vanished.

Coco looked at me. "Room service is at the door, Johnny. Shall I let them in?"

I nodded and the door clicked open. A young guy wearing a black bow tie and a red waistcoat pushed in a trolley with an ice bucket on it and three glasses. Two gold foiled necks poked out of the mountain of chipped ice. The waiter didn't glance at the two beauties frolicking on the bed.

"Shall I pour, sir?"

I nodded and he popped the cork discretely into a napkin, poured three fizzing streams, then bowed and retreated. I picked up two glasses and approached the bed. Astrid was panting, her cheeks flushed and her T-shirt had ridden up to expose one breast, pale pink nipple barely darker than her lightly tanned skin. Sigrid's hair was plastered over her face. She pulled it back from her eyes with two fingers and looked at me, her lips parting as she breathed.

"Ladies," I said, handing them each a glass before fetching mine. "Here's a toast. To Marcus Goldenrod, the best pal I guy could ever want for."

"To Marcus!"

They slurped the champagne, Sigrid spilling it down her chin and Astrid rubbing the underside of her nose with a knuckle.

"It tickles!"

A little silence passed between us as Barry reached a crescendo and the track faded away. The next track started with simple strings and as he belted out his first notes Sigrid giggled at me.

"Don't get cold feet! My feet are too hot!" She wiggled her toes through the open front of her boots. "Help me get them off, Johnny."

I loved the way she made my name sound, exotic, foreign. *Yonny*, something like that.

I took hold of the ankle and heel of her proffered leg and tugged. Sigrid squealed and wiggled her toes so more. I dragged her along the bed more than getting the boot away from her, but eventually it popped off. By the time I had its partner removed she was practically off the bed. She slid the rest of the way and knelt before me.

"Did you like us rubbing against you when we danced?"

"Yes. Yes I did."

Her hand was on my thigh, you know, the thick thigh, and it began to twitch as she rubbed up and down its length. My breathing grew shallow until I was interrupted by Astrid drumming her heels against the bed.

147

"My toes are hot too! Do me next!"

Astrid didn't even try to stay on the bed and laid on the carpet, leg in the air, before I even had her first boot off. As I tugged on the second her foot joined Sigrid's hand on my thigh.

"Have you ever dreamed about being with twins, Johnny?" Astrid foot rocked against my base and Sigrid's palm stroked my tip.

"Why are you still dressed, Johnny?" Sigrid peeled off her clinging T-shirt and looked up at me, raising her pale brown eyebrows, a vision of Scandinavian perfection. Genes of Sweden; I salute you.

I tossed my jacket onto the sofa and the girls clapped.

"Dance for us! Like in the disco!"

I started to move in time with the ballad, remembering Bianca's reaction to my moves, then looking at the blonde models at my feet, clapping and giggling. What did Bianca know anyway? She might know her Beethoven from her Bach, but she knew nothing about the rhythmic animal magnetism exuded by my primal dance energy.

"More!" Astrid wriggled her way out of the rest of her top, threw it at me and I brought it to my face, breathed deeply her hot, damp scent of flowers and spice. I unbuttoned my shirt, spread it to the appreciative whoops of the twins then cast it behind me with a flourish.

Sigrid's hands were on my belt buckle, and Astrid pulled the strap through. The button, the zip, then they pulled my trousers down. The girls looked at each other, giggled, then together reached for my shorts and pulled them down. I sprung to attention and there was a squeal of delight from the twins.

"Johnny," said Sigrid, a little breathlessly. "Is it okay if we take it in turns? You can tell us who does it best!"

My heart pounded and I nodded. Sigrid's lips enclosed me in a warm rush of giddy pleasure, Astrid stroking her sister's hair away from her face and whispering in Swedish to her. My eyes closed and my head fell back.

This was the best day of my life.

I had no doubt that I wasn't the first guy to be on the receiving end of this orchestrated assault. As Sigrid sucked me Astrid encouraged her to take me deeper, squeezing my butt cheeks and making me rock my hips to match her sister's bobbing.

"My turn," Astrid said, nudging Sigrid's shoulder who pulled off me with long, slow suction that made me groan.

Astrid started working me faster, alternating strokes of her grasping hand that brought me nearer to the edge with lip floggings that sent me to a dreamy zone of bliss. She seemed intent on some sweet sadism, to bring me to the brink then lead me away, two worlds of pleasure, tributaries flowing and joining as one.

"Not too soon," said Sigrid, and Astrid released me, contenting herself with running the tip of her tongue along my shaft as my chest heaved.

Sigrid kissed my tip, pressing it against her yielding lips, smearing it against her until most of her lipstick had wiped off and I was glossed with her bright pink. She giggled, nipped me gently and stood up.

Astrid kissed the side of my shaft and joined her. Without their heels the girls still had an inch on me. They held hands, naked apart from their tiny blue shorts and smiled at me.

"So," said Sigrid. "Who was better?"

"I..." I flushed, and I stammered, and I looked from one of them to the other; four bright blue eyes looking back at me. "It's so hard to say. I mean you were both... incredible, sexy, beautiful... I can't say—"

"He means it's a draw," said Astrid. "We need to go to the next round."

"The next round?" They each took my hand and placed it on their hip. "Oh, I see."

I tugged on their shorts and they wriggled their hips to help me. It was actually harder than you might think; they were really tight shorts and they had plump little tushies. I resorted to using both hands on Astrid to yank them past her ass and almost expected a popping sound when they came off. She stepped out of them and kicked them away and I looked up those ski slope legs to the pale brown wisp between them.

"He picked me first," said Astrid, dancing on the spot with her hands in little fists above her head.

Sigrid squealed and stamped her foot. She barged Astrid out of the way with her hips and her sister fell back onto the bed, laughing. Sigrid frowned at me and her bottom lip was sticking out.

"Well?" Her arms were crossed over her lovely breasts, and with a pang I realized that I missed them.

"Sorry, it's just that I was struggling to do you both at once so I just sort of let go one hand to do it with both hands and I didn't pick one of you I just—"

Sigrid stamped her foot again and I eased her shorts past her equally plump tushie. She stepped out of them, turned her back on me and went and sat on the far side of the bed.

"Sisi... come on..."

Astrid rolled across the sheets reaching for her sister with one hand and beckoning me with the other.

"You're being mean again, Sassa. You always do this." Sigrid voice was thick and choked.

"Come on, Sisi. You know I was just having fun, I didn't mean anything, I promise."

Astrid crawled over to her sister touched her on the shoulder. Sigrid flinched her shoulder away, her head tilting forward as she hunched there naked. Astrid put both arms around her, hugging her as Sigrid first tried to shake her loose, then shaking more as she started crying.

"Hush, hush." Astrid stroked her sister's hair and slowly the sobbing subsided.

"I liked him more than you. You knew that," Sigrid said.

"And here he is," Astrid said, lifting up her sister's chin and turning it to me.

Sigrid's already smeared mascara had spidery trails down her cheeks, and her eyes were pink. I poured two more glasses.

"I think," I said handing the girls the drinks, "the problem is too much tequila and too little champagne. Can we blame Mexico, forgive everyone else, then just kiss and make up?"

Sigrid sniffled. Then a little smile, then a bigger one. She turned to her sister and kissed her in a gentle private way then they clashed glasses and drained them. I could have happily stood and watched them kiss for a bit longer but Sigrid fell back onto the bed and held her arms out for me. The light tan on her long limbs, breasts squeezed together, nipples erect, her blue eyes, her pink lips, mouth half open, you can't resist that, not for longer than a moment.

I dropped into her arms and she squeezed me as our lips met. Electric surprise after her teasing on the dance floor.

Her tongue flicked against mine and she drew my hand up the side of her body, released it, and I continued the journey of exploration. She pulled away and giggled as I pushed past her arm pit then took my head in her hands and kissed me again.

I felt a shock as another pair of lips kissed my shoulder, nipped at me and another hand on my back, spiraling and stroking, moving lower to the curve of my spine, grabbing hold of my ass. Astrid was starting to play.

My cock was trapped between my belly and Sigrid, hot and pulsing, and as her passion grew she parted her legs. I raised myself up onto my knees with some difficulty as Sigrid wouldn't release my head. She chewed gently on my bottom lip, the bed rocked as Astrid got up.

Sigrid pushed my head down her body, against her breasts,

moaning as her stiff pale nipples rubbed across my face. I took one into my mouth, playing with it between my teeth, then released it as I gasped. Astrid had my cock in her hand and it twitched at her touch. She was behind me, cupping my balls with her other hand. I felt the tightness of a rubber against my tip, then the compression of it being rolled up. I thanked its reduction in sensation, praying that I'd last long enough to manage both of them.

Between my legs, Astrid guided my cock, pressed against my buttocks, and Sigrid's thighs parted further and she let out a long moan as I penetrated her. Just the tip, then more and more until I had fully hilted myself and she groaned with each stroke.

Astrid released my balls and walked around the bed until she stood opposite me. Her smile was wicked and one eye creased in a roguish half-wink. She lifted her hair up from her neck, held it piled on top of her head, turned her chin from side to side as she held my gaze. The diamond formed by her arms, the double swell of her breasts at the bottom and her framed beautiful, teasing face. I looked back down at Sigrid, moaning open mouthed, lashes fluttering and her mascara-stained cheeks. She was raw emotion, out of control, Astrid was tempered and dangerous. It was glorious.

"Can you handle both of us at once? Will you last?"

Astrid knelt on the bed, her knees apart. Her arms trailed down, down her neck and across her breasts. Blonde strands cascaded around her face and she held out two fingers to me, stroking my lips then putting the tips in my mouth. I sucked them and she let out a small cry, and I took them deeper, sucking her like she had done to me.

She put her fingers between her legs, parting her lips and smiling at my involuntary puff of desire. Astrid began to stroke herself, her belly arching and her other hand teasing her nipple. Sigrid's moans grew louder and she began to quiver and yelp softly. I ground against her and she cried out, clutching my hips so I moved harder against her as she came and she spasmed tightly around my shaft.

I was too near release and I stopped thrusting, tried to breathe evenly, letting the excitement fade just a bit and last a bit longer. Sigrid pulled my head down, touching her lips to mine, mumbling soft Swedish words. I couldn't understand her but knew what she was communicating.

Her eyes opened gazing at me as her ribs subsided. Astrid's hand was on my shoulder, urging me to the side.

"Roll over, Johnny. It's my turn."

I fell onto my side, pulling away from Sigrid who moaned her protestation.

"Hush, Siri," Astrid said. "He can do more for you."

Sigrid propped herself up on her elbows as the bed rocked again and Astrid clambered over me. First a kiss on my forehead, then her lips on mine for the first time. She bit my chin then dragged her breasts across my face as she kissed my chest; bit my nipples, one after the other. She kept crawling, I felt her nipples running down my body, I raised my chin to kiss her belly as it passed. Astrid's thighs were either side of my head and I could smell her sex, glistening above my lips, then against my lips. I licked her and she sighed, taking my cock in her hand and squeezing around its base.

She tasted different than Bianca, different than Raquel. Sweet, almost like melon and cinnamon and I moved the tip of my tongue against her button, pushing back against the tiny pucker of her hood. Astrid's hips turned, presenting more of herself to me. Her lips parted as I licked deeper, entering her with my tongue. Her grip on my cock tightened so I delved deeper, pressing my face to her as she flowered open, bucking her hips in short twists and panting each time I penetrated her.

Abruptly Astrid stopped, rolled of me and let go of my cock.

"Oh he is wonderful, Siri. You must try him," she said.

I just lay there as Sigrid took her sister's position and Astrid climbed over my hips, guiding my cock into her and blowing gently between pursed lips as she descended my slick pole. Astrid flipped her hips, grinding against the last inch of me and I licked Sigrid, taking hold of her cheeks and spreading them so I could get my tongue deeper inside her.

With Sigrid's button on my tongue and Astrid gyrating on my cock I felt our pulses were connected, an upward slope as our tempo slowly rose together. Sigrid's soft yelps getting closer together, Astrid leaning back, gripping my thighs so she could push harder against me, take me deeper inside me and we reached a place together, a perfect high note ringing through our bodies, and we came together. Ecstatic white volcano unloading into Astrid, her clamping around me as she spasmed and Sigrid squealing as the waves of pleasure took her.

I drifted on the edge of sleep. Sluggish movements from Sigrid, climbing off me, curling up next to me and pulling the sheet over us. Astrid lying down beside me, a soft moan as I slipped from inside her.

If it was the end of my time now, then I was ready to go. Nothing on my list had ever anticipated such a moment. Sigrid's head on my shoulder, her hair trailed on my face. Astrid kissed my cheek and laid her head beside mine and her hand on my chest. Content and satisfied and spent and warm, and feeling that I truly deserved this, I slept.

Chapter 12: Suicide Day

Six Years Ago

Smalltown Town Mall

I need to take you on one last flashback. Forgive me, no more after this. You can use the fade to black of the previous scene, whatever suits you. You're now looking at a younger Johnny. It's midday, clear and sunny, and it's my eighteenth birthday. I'm also standing on the edge of the roof of *Freddy's* the town mall, hardly more than a three story department store, but we called it the mall. I'm some thirty feet above the street. I chose this spot because last year an old guy came here when he lost his job at the steel mill after working there thirty years. And he did the exact same thing I'm planning to do.

The last few years have not been easy on me. I don't have any friends anymore. Whether they abandoned me or I pushed them away, well it doesn't really matter anymore. My only social interaction came when my mother would make me take soup next door to Mrs. Podenski. Mrs. Podenski was ninety-seven years old, wheelchair-bound and frail, but had a loving, warm, all-embracing goodness that seeped even through the shell of misery I had accreted around me.

She would tell me stories about the old country, as she called it. About Ralph, her husband, gone over twenty years now; how handsome he was and how much they loved each other. She said I was a good boy to spend so much time listening to the stories of an old woman, but that I lit up her day and it warmed her soul more than my mother's soup.

High school is hell. You've heard that before. For me it was a living hell, true enough. I don't know why they kept picking on me day after day. I didn't even fight back. If I was tripped up I just lay there, listening to the taunts until they went away. Several times girls tricked me, asking me on dates then cackling with all their cronies when I turned up at parties only to have the door slammed in my face.

Even Gwen Hertzensbrecher tried to do it, usually once a year. She'd come over to some empty area of the yard where I'd be sitting alone with my sandwiches. She'd say, "Hey, we never hang out any more. Remember when we said we'd be friends forever? What happened to that?" I'd walk away without a word, leaving her calling after me. I knew it was another lie, and it hurt me more than all the others because all I wanted to do was to take her in my arms and tell that we could go back to that happy time. She was a pretty girl, sure, but that wasn't what made her special. It was her smile. A smile that lit up the world, filled it with her presence, made everything it fell upon feel special and magical and unique. Why did the girl with that smile— the girl I loved—have to be so cruel?

I tried, for a while, to take the bus to neighboring towns, hang out at parks or coffee shops and meet other kids. Well, girls mostly. It worked sometimes too. I'd get friendly with a girl, start making regular weekend dates to go over and see her; all the time a little sparkle of light growing inside me as I started to hope that this might be the one. Things would warm up, holding hands as we walked, a kiss on the cheek at the end of a date, a kiss on the lips at the beginning of the next. Each time however there would come a time, be it the backseat of my old man's car, or some secluded picnic spot, when they would reach for my zipper, take a look beneath then it would be a flip of a coin whether they'd run away laughing or screaming.

I'd turned off the alarm as I woke on my eighteenth birthday, crossed my hands behind my head and stared at the ceiling, wondering how this year might be different from the last four. I turned options over in my head and eventually came to the conclusion that it would not. I'd thought about suicide before; ah heck, I'll admit it. I'd read up on different ways to do it, which were quick and painless or which ones if they got you to a hospital quick enough might fail. The idea of suicide was something I kept as a secret hope. It was something that let me endure the pain because I knew there was a way out. I knew that if it got too unbearable I'd just kill myself. In some way clinging onto it actually made things worse and I got deeper and deeper into my depression without cracking on the surface, or anyone else finding out how bad I'd got.

I wrote a note for my parents. Telling them why I did it, and not to blame themselves, but there was nothing they could have done and they didn't understand, would never understand what it had been like for me.

So I stood there, the toes of my Chuck Taylor All Star's just over the edge. Looking down as customers came and went, parking in the wide lot out front, and pushing shopping carts back and forth. I wanted it to be somewhere public. I hoped someone would feel sorry for me. I hoped at school they'd feel guilty; see what it meant when you turned someone's life—a real person's life—into nothing more than a running gag.

I was crying and the pain in my chest was so bad I thought I was dying right as I stood there. My shoulders shook as I bawled and as I reached the shriek of self-loathing and despising the world I threw myself off the roof.

* * *

I became dimly aware of a light and of muffled voice. I felt like I was floating, cocooned in a numb stasis, then I slipped into sleep. When I next awoke the light was much brighter and I squinted against it. I felt people moving around me, voices less muffled but still not forming words. I think I slept again then. Sometime after that I felt the pain. My legs ached, my sides throbbed and when I twitched my fingers lances of fire ran into my arms.

It took several days but as they reduced my morphine dosage my mind became clearer. My parents were there, my mother's nose pink with a tissue pressed to it, her eyes bloodshot; my father's forehead knitted and wrinkled with his arm around mom. Everyone was so worried about me, they said, but I didn't need to worry about anything else ever again. My father said that it would be okay, that he'd take care of things from now on, and that he loved me very much.

How did I survive? I managed to croak the question but I think my jaw had been wired shut. My mom started crying and looked to the doctor for support. It was Mrs. Podenski, he said. She had been out in her electric wheelchair, picking up a few things from the store. She broke my fall, her and the wheelchair. I tried to ask—is she? What little voice I had was getting choked as the horrifying guilt welled up inside me. The doctor shook his head, said he was sorry.

I think they must have put me back on the morphine then. I don't remember anything else for a while. Sometime later I remember being wheeled back from operations to remove pins, and later on trying to balance on crutches and walking braces. Twelve weeks, they said, if I was lucky. It took longer as I listlessly refused to exercise, wallowing in the grey mist of prescription meds and apathy. I felt nothing anymore. Even my one chance of escape was gone. How could I attempt suicide if something horrific like what I did to Mrs. Podenski could happen again?

They moved me to a special care facility, kept me on a pretty assortment of colored pills. I had daily counseling as they worked on what they called 'my issues'. There were other guys there and girls too. We were all classified as 'high risk to ourselves or others'. Our bedrooms didn't have doors and there were cameras everywhere. They made us play 'trust your buddy games', falling back into the arms of strangers.

I guess something they did worked because after about two months they discharged me. My parents were waiting and they drove me away. A new start, my father said. This family needs a new start. He asked if I'd ever thought about living in the Big City. It must be stifling for a kid, he said, to live their whole life in a small town.

True to his word, we moved. A new life in the Big City. Big enough that you could be a stranger to everyone if you wanted to and I wrapped myself in the duvet of anonymity. I went through college without making friends, but Big City College was a mix of kids, immigrants getting an education, people taking diplomas to get along in their job, early moms finishing high school. No-one noticed me and I preferred it that way.

We're right about where you and I met and I started telling you my tale. So why am I telling you this right now? Well, by the time I told you about Astrid and Ingrid you might have started to think things were going too easy for me. That I'd had a winning streak that had gone on too long. I want you to think again on what it had been like for me up 'till then.

As far as I'm concerned I deserved every bit of outrageous good luck that came my way this final day.

Chapter 13: Ebola Girl

10:51 pm

I startled myself awake. What time was it? Sigrid mumbled as I rolled her head off my chest and she pulled the sheet tighter around her shoulder. Astrid's breath whispered between her lips so I moved slowly, inching my way down the bed.

I picked up my jacket, found The List which hadn't been updated since before Bianca, and found I now could finally cross off that troublesome one, along with a minor one that had gone on The List when I was starting to run out of great ideas and had managed all the ones a sexually frustrated twenty-one year old could come up with.

~~Number 11: Have a threesome with two girls~~
~~Number 26: Sample fine champagne~~

Sleepy Swedish mumbles drew my attention back to the Bröstenberg twins. Something a special as this deserved more than just a single strikethrough.

~~Number 32: Bone twins, at the same time~~

Technically, I suppose you could accuse me of cheating as you couldn't do Number 31 without Number 11, but this was my game, I had about seven hours left, and I made the rules.

Marcus' private en suite had a computerized console for the shower that took me a couple of minutes to work out. I wanted a simple 'warm water comes out the top and covers you then drains away' type of shower but it looked like I needed to have to turn off each side spout and individual steam pump before I could use it.

As I finished, shaking my hair and reaching for a towel, one was placed in my hand. I dried off my face and looked up and Astrid and Sigrid, coiling around the door frame like sexual Swedish serpents.

"We thought you might stay longer," said Astrid.

"Please, Johnny, just another hour?" Sigrid's makeup had become even messier as she'd slept.

I continued toweling as they squeezed past me and climbed into the shower together. I started the side jets and could hear them squealing above the rushing of the shower. I was puzzled with myself; why would I want to leave? Why would any sane (and straight) man want to leave? It couldn't just be The List. So much had happened today I no longer felt that I owed it to myself to cross of everything or as much as I could before I went. I'd had experiences that most men never achieve, so what was it that I felt was lacking?

I didn't know, I just knew it wasn't in here with the never-mind how delectable nympho twins.

I dressed and wandered back to the bathroom as I did up my shirt buttons. The shower door was open and a soapy Sigrid was lathering Astrid's shoulders.

"Don't you want to join us, Johnny?" Sigrid pursed her pretty lips at me.

I shook my head. "Ladies, you are adorable, magnificent, and delicious. This is something I'll remember for the rest of my life. May I?" I held up my phone.

The Bröstenberg twins giggled and pressed their foam covered bodies together. The flash went off and I had it immortalized. In a world that made any kind of sense it should have been a centerfold.

I bowed, Astrid blew a palmful of foam at me then they returned the business of giggling and soaping each other.

I sighed and smiled at the same time. I didn't know what I was doing but I knew it was right. I felt sure that somewhere the Master was shaking his finger at me, but I didn't care.

The breakneck urgency of my day seemed greatly relieved and I wandered back down the stairs to the party with no real plan, other than if I bumped into Marcus I could thank him, fervently, and return his key to him.

The pumping music rose to greet me as I approached, the trebles and the lead line resolving themselves as I entered the bar. The barman gave me a grin and by the time I'd made it out to the party side he was laying a paper coaster on the bar and setting another martini on it, gestured to it with a wave of his palm, then was off to take another order.

My nap had refreshed me and I took a look at the dance floor as I reapplied alcohol to my system. I'd had nothing to eat apart from a sandwich in the morning, some fruit later on, and a small salad of cocktail olives over the course of the day. The martini glowed in me and I felt the music seeping into me, the beat calling me to embrace it and join the heaving throng.

"Hi..." came a husky voice to my right, hot breath on my ear.

She was black, beautiful and busty. Her full lips quivered as her lashes fluttered. Her hair was bleached to bronze and her skin looked like chocolate dusted with gold powder. The pink bikini top only barely contained her impressive boobs, with a long bead necklace resting between them, and she had on white clubbing shorts that had been slashed up to the hips at each side. If she had been in heels she'd have been taller than me but she had on simple sandals with more beads strung around each ankle.

Swaying her hips in time with the music, she danced a slowly turning pirouette, wiggled her ass at me and then laughed.

"You not dancing anymore, sugar? I saw you dancing with those skinny blonde twins earlier, and I have to say boy, you got moves."

"Heh, thank you. Just taking a break, you know, getting some energy back after... well..."

Her eyes widened. "Both of them? Sugar, you must be alright."

I rocked my glass at her. "Join me for a drink?"

She leaned on the bar beside me, placing her hand on the sleeve of my jacket, casually.

"I saw you with Marcus too. Is he a friend of yours?"

I had an idea where this was going and I liked it. "School friend actually. We go back a way. You?"

"I come to his parties; it's pretty easy to get in if... you know?" Her fingertip tucked her hair behind her ear, traced her large hoop earring.

"You mean if you are drop dead gorgeous?"

She fluttered her lashes again and touched her neck. "You think I'm gorgeous?"

"I think you're drop dead gorgeous."

She smiled and held out her hand. "Nice to meet you, I'm Zoey. Zoey Beaver."

I knew enough now not to have a drink at my lips when a strange girl told me her name. I took her fingers in my hand and puffed a faint kiss on them.

"I'm Johnny. Johnny Johnson."

"My, what a gentleman. You're much nicer than most of the guys here. Your aura positively glows white. What do you say we go somewhere a bit quieter where we can talk?"

I knew she was trying to get closer to Marcus and that I looked like a way in. I'm not that dumb. I just didn't care.

"Sounds great—where?"

"My place? I've got some great organic wine just delivered today. It would be terribly cruel of you to make me drink it alone."

Game on, Johnny.

Zoey walked through the dancers, the curve of her hips an alluring shape to follow. Her figure was fuller than any of the women I'd known today and I felt a fierce desire to hold her and trace those curves with my hands. She looked over her shoulder to see if I was following, saw me checking out her ass and laughed, touching the side of her neck again.

The Master had said to watch their necks, the unconscious invitation, and she was fairly shouting it.

As we passed through the main party hall the crowd had thinned considerably. A white haired guy in a tux was crooning old Frank Sinatra numbers and a dozen couples were clasped and rotating beneath the bandstand. Only a few red waistcoats still mingled amongst the remaining guests and the buffet tables which had been laid out with canapés were empty and being dismantled by two men in janitorial overalls. I looked for Marcus or Bianca but saw neither. Zoey held out her hand and we went out and down the great stairs together.

"I'll get my car," I said, heading for the valet who was sitting on the bottom stair and playing with his phone.

Zoey tugged me back. "You're swaying a bit too much to drive, baby. Taxi!"

One pulled up to the curb as she waved her arm and she bundled me inside. She gave the driver instruction, he grumbled and we started on our way.

"It's only a few minutes away," Zoey said. "Want me to tell your future? I'm a tiny bit psychic, you know? My grandmother could tell everything about someone, just by looking at them. That's why I said hi to you at the party. You have such delicate white aura. I knew you were nice. I'm very good at reading people."

She took my hand and ran her thumb across my palm. She frowned and pulled it closer to her face, angling it to catch the flickers of passing streetlights.

"Hmm. That's odd, I've never seen that on someone before."

"What is it?"

"Your life line. It just, kind of stops. Weird."

That figures.

"Zoey," I said. "You seem like a great girl, but I don't want to give you the wrong impression. I'm not really into, um, commitment. You see I—"

"Silly boy." She released my hand and stroked my cheek. "Commitment is something that happens or doesn't happen. You can build trust with someone slowly or not at all, but that depends on both of you. I believe that being with another person, sharing the joy and intimacy of that moment doesn't have to be about marriage. Laws should have nothing to do with it—it's none of the government's business what I decide to do with my own body or with who. You get it?"

"You mean free love?"

"Right on, sugar!" She put her hand on my thigh (the regular one) and moved closer to me. "You don't think it makes me a slut if I want to engage in a mutually consenting activity with another open minded adult, do you?"

"Absolutely not, I—"

She closed her eyes and kissed me, the pillowy crush of her lips overwhelming me and unlike any of the other girls. Her hand moved up my leg but the taxi stopped and he tooted his horn. She broke away from the kiss, biting onto her bottom lip. My arm was trapped under her but she paid the fare and pulled me out the taxi.

Her apartment was in a recently restored brownstone, neat grey steps with wrought-iron handrails leading up to doors framed by a carved stone arch with the relief of a bearded man carved in the capstone.

I don't remember much about the dark hall and stairs as she pressed those wonderful lips against mine again and we stumbled up the stairs, grasping each other, feeling for the wall and tripping on steps.

"Wait a moment, sugar."

We stopped outside a door that was only greyly lit by the window at the end on the hall. Zoey's purse jangled as she searched within it then she unlocked the door.

"Come on in, quietly."

I padded into her apartment as she lit a couple of candles. The hall was painted a dusty green and opened into a living room that had pink walls, but almost every inch of it was covered by ethnic weavings and patterned cloth. She had a penchant for sixties posters and, what I believe a male psychiatrist would agree, something of an obsession for cushions, which were a motley collection of tribal styles from across the planet.

"This was my grandmother's place. She was a real swinger back in the day, but she looked after me in when I moved to the city. It's mine now, bless her."

"It's great," I said. "Very... bohemian."

"Just a moment while I check something," Zoey said.

She tapped lightly on a closed door that lead from the living room, waited, and after getting no response she opened it and stuck her head inside.

"She's out," Zoey said closing the door and smiling at me. "That means we don't need to be quiet then, does it?"

"Oh right... Oh! I see."

"So..." She started to ease my jacket off my shoulders. "Do you want to do it on the couch or in the bedroom?"

I could feel my body reacting to her heat, wanting to explore those delicious curves, but I'd had enough scares today to have learned a bit of caution.

"Your roommate, is she by any chance a bit crazy? Maybe into bondage or something like that? Does she and... I mean do both of you... ahem.... I mean together—"

Zoey tossed her hair back and chuckled. "I wish... mmm... but no, sorry, she's squeaky clean. Poor little thing. She's so secretive I think she mighta actually have made up the guy she's dating. Why do you ask, you into that kind of thing?"

"Me? No! It's just that... ah forget it. Where's your bedroom?"

Zoey had my jacket off and draped it over her shoulder as she turned.

"This way, sugar."

She kicked off her sandals after she closed the door behind us, wandering around lighting candles and scented sticks. Her room was just like the living room but she had more of the ethnic printed sheets draped from ceiling hooks making a tent over the bed. There was a dusty guitar in the corner with a couple of strings missing, and the strong smell of incense couldn't mask the lingering residue of weed.

"Lend me a hand, will ya?"

Zoey had her back to me and was trying to reach the tie of her bikini top. I brushed her hair to the side and kissed her at the base of her neck. She sighed and her head rolled back, exposing her neck to more kisses. Her hands came up and held my head so I kept nibbling there and she moaned as I did it.

I undid the tie behind her neck and let the strings slip between my fingers, then undid the final knot behind her back and the bikini top fell down. My hands rested on her hips, soft as I squeezed them, pulled her back to me, hardening as I rubbed myself against her plump booty.

"Ooo," Zoey said. "I can feel you..."

She arched her back and started to flip her hips, then wriggled from side to side, then combined it in a figure eight. I pinched her, gently, on each side, delighting in how her flesh compressed under my fingers. The stroking from her dance moves made me thicken with desire. I slid my hands up her flanks, forward, then cupped her swaying breasts, feeling her nipples harden against my palms. Zoey panted, a little gasp each time I ran my fingers past her stiffening flesh. Her areola felt so wide as it began to pucker, her nipples as long as the first joint of my little finger.

"Yes," she sighed. "You can do it a little bit harder... yes..."

Zoey turned abruptly, her eyes slitted and her lips swollen; she took me by the head and kissed me hard, flicking the tip of her tongue into my mouth. She broke away, started tearing at my shirt buttons.

The shirt hit the floor followed shortly by my belt. I wobbled on one leg pulling my shoe off and she released me, parting the diaphanous curtain over the bed revealing messed up sheets and more pillows that were untidily tumbled across the mattress.

I had one shoe on and my pants around my knees when she stopped me with a finger under my chin and raised me to stand straight. Zoey held her arms above her head, then ran them down across her breasts, into the front of her little white shorts, then hooked her thumbs at the side of them, pressing them down past her hip bones until a frill of black hair was visible. My pulse roared in my ear like hearing the sea.

Watching me the whole time, Zoey smiled, moving her shoulders closer together to squeeze those magnificent brown boobs together, and her areola like double chocolate cookies. She moved the shorts a tiny bit lower, more black hair and I my lips parted as the desire for her rose uncontrollably within me. Just when she had the waistband at the widest point of her hips, she stopped. I think I made some kind of sound in my throat because she grinned and shuffled around, rolling her hips like she had when she had been grinding on me.

A darker shadow on the delicious chocolate of her back ran down her spine, at the end a crack where her cheeks were squeezed together. At the base of her spine she had a tattoo of Sanskrit letters spelling *aum*. I wanted to reach out and grab her ass cheeks, squeeze them, bite them. She kept rolling her hips and began again to tantalizingly slowly move them down, the bisector growing, until both cheeks popped free, jiggling with her movements.

I groaned, feeling that I couldn't hold back any longer.

"Zoey..." I said.

"I wondered how long you could last, sugar." She giggled, shook loose her shorts, stepped out of them and turned around, holding her arms out for me.

Wow. That was the biggest bush I'd seen all day. Serves me right for going home with a hippie.

She followed my gaze and ran her fingers through the luxuriant grove.

"You taking a fondness to my patch, Johnny?"

Guys, none of you would have done anything different. She was beautiful, had an awesome body, she was naked and she wanted me. I wasn't going to worry about scrambling through some brush to get to the picnic.

I grabbed her, pulled her onto the bed and she squealed, rolling me over and struggling to get my pants past my ankles. We were both giggling until she started on getting my shorts down.

"Oh Johnny!"

"Yeah..." I flicked the foil wrapper aside and grinned.

"Be gentle with me..."

"Hush, Zoey. I'm going to take good care of you."

Yesterday I could never have imagined being calm around a woman, never mind such a gorgeous and alluring one, but after a day like today, well, it changes you. At least it did for me.

I teased her with my tip, then took it away. I crawled up and down her body licking her, kissing her, nipping her with my teeth. She shuddered when I took her nipples between my lips, pulled my head to her so I would work them harder, then I entered her fully and she made little groans, cut off when her breath caught in her throat at the end of each deep thrust.

I started to increase my tempo, to take her to new heights, but she gripped me hard by the wrist.

"Don't hurry, take your time, please..."

A strand of a Prince ballad ran through my mind and I shuddered.

"What's wrong, sugar?"

"Nothing... I just... it's nothing, I'm fine. What were you saying?"

Zoey wrapped her legs around me, denying me movement but rolling her hips; rubbing her button against me. I felt her bush tickling my abdomen.

"Just go slow, Johnny, it's not a race. Have you heard of *tantra?*"

I had but only had the vaguest idea what it might mean. I figured that she might teach me a thing or two so it would probably be better to play along.

"No I haven't. What is it?"

"Oh sugar, you are so naive. Tantra is a mystical art developed over thousands of years ago in India. It's the study of pleasure... *oh...*"

Her eyelashes fluttered as she gave her lecture. Zoey seemed perfectly at ease writhing about, pinioned by my pole, while having a chat at the same time. I tugged on her long brown nipples and she moaned, then bundled me over so I was on my back and she was astride me, pressing my hands against her breasts.

"Tantra teaches us to prolong the feelings of pleasure, to explore... *oh... oh...* explore the world of the senses... *oh Johnny...* to reach new heights by delaying climax."

I wasn't sure I was learning anything but I was very sure I didn't want her to stop. She drew the edges of her nails down my chest and tweaked my nipples, tugging them as I had done to her.

"The highest forms of tantra use the overload of pleasure, the perfect state the human body can attain... *oh... oh...* and heal terrible psychological scars or even diseases themselves."

"You can heal... *uh...* diseases with sex?"

It was distracting, sure, but while I wasn't racing for the finish line I found it wasn't that hard to stay aroused, enjoy her and even talk with her. I guess it's a bit like taking one hand off the steering wheel and glancing at the scenery as you go past.

"Sure... *oh...* you can, sugar... *oh my...* it's part of the medical system in Europe I've been told... *oh...* and there are several clinics in this state alone."

Why hadn't Dr. Yu considered this? It sounded at least plausible, worth a go, after all, I'd didn't have anything to lose and it wasn't anything like facing up to a big syringe.

"So, how does it... *uh... uh...* work then?"

I pushed her back and got to my knees at the same time. I pulled her knees up beside me, entering her again. Zoey's head lolled off the end of the bed and she moaned deeply as I resumed fucking her.

"Well, I guess that it's different for... *oh God yes keep doing that Johnny it's amazing...*different for different cases. People react differently to different medications, don't they? This is... *oh yes...* is just the same thing. For me it only took about half an hour... *oh harder Johnny oh...* half an hour, which the doctor said was lucky because he had ... *oh... oh...* another appointment then."

I stopped poling her and she squealed, raising her head and pouting those beautiful big lips at me.

"What?" I said.

"You don't have to stop completely if you think you are going to blow, Johnny. Just think about... *mmm...* just one of the sensations, explore it, enjoy it in isolation. Learn to recognize your own pleasure. Try it, sugar. Try moving slowly and don't rush it."

I took up the slow bucking and her head fell back again with a groan. Zoey rolled her nipples between her thumb and fingers, making little gasps as she tugged them at the end of each stroke I made.

"What was... *uh...* that bit about the doctor again?"

"Last year I was having a routine... *oh yes oh...* routine checkup, and the doctor found something wrong. He was a very experienced doctor in his... *oh...* his sixties, and he'd done everything very... *oh...* thoroughly, making me take off all my clothes and literally examining... *oh...* every inch of my body... *oh Johnny just a little faster oh yes sugar oh yes...* but when he had finished I could see... *mmm yes...* see something was wrong in his face. He told me I had Ebola and I would—"

I stopped moving again. "Wait, what? You had Ebola?"

Zoey's ankles locked behind my back again and she drew me hard against her, hilting myself fully in her. She moaned and arched her back and I put my arm under her to pull her back onto the bed. I rolled her over to that her beautiful brown tushie was accessible, spread her legs and lightly spanked her bottom. I moved forward, penetrating her, enjoying the brush of her chunky cheeks against my groin as I pressed against her.

She clutched at the sheets as I resumed my gentle rhythmic rocking.

"You were saying about Ebola," I said.

"Yeah... *oh yeah oh oh...* so the doctor said it was terrible, but his tests showed I had Ebola and that I was going to... *mmm yes baby yes...* going to die within the hour. Naturally I broke down in tears and... *oh...* and begged him that there had to be something he could do. I was too young and pretty to die. Well he... *oh yeah just like that baby just like oh...* he said the only thing that stood a sliver of a chance would be tantric sex and there was barely enough time left to even attempt it. It was the only chance to get my sero... sero-something—"

"Serotonin?"

"Yeah, that's it. Well I begged him... *oh... oh...* and bless his dedicated medical heart, he agreed and we got down to it straight away in the examination room."

"What happened?"

Zoey half rolled onto her side, one leg between mine and crooking the other around my hip. I held her knee in one hand and took a good handful of her ass in the other. This was some kind of weird scissor position I hadn't come across despite being such an avid consumer of porn, but Zoey's eyes kept rolling up as I went deep within her so I guessed I was hitting the right spot somewhere.

"Well, it was kind of like we are... *ooo yes baby right there uh-huh oh...* he said it was important to try as many positions as possible so

179

we had the best chance of stopping the disease and, bless him, by the end I was worried for his heart, the dear sweet old man. He tried so hard to... *oh...oh...* to save my live that it nearly cost him his own. Finally when he had blown his load over my face he bent down, took a close look at me and clapped his hands. He... *oh keep hitting it there oh God it feels so good...* he said that I was cured and that it was a miracle I could go about my normal life... *oh...* as if nothing had happened. I kissed that sweet shy old man on his little bald forehead and from that day on I've studied tantra myself."

This was incredible! Surely cancer is just as serious a disease as Ebola—maybe I had a chance!

"Zoey, I... need to tell you something... *uh... uh...* I'm dying. I have terminal cancer and have, well about six or so hours to live."

Her hand covered her mouth as she gasped. "Oh my God, Johnny. That's terrible! But that... *oh yeah grind it baby...* that explains what I saw when I read your palm. You poor baby!"

"But can't I be cured as well?"

I was really enjoying the sensation of her butt slapping against my thigh with each stroke and I focused on it, the rhythm, the soft warmth of her skin hitting me, how the warmth spread across my leg as her cheek did the same, the moment of coolness as we parted, a microsecond of regret before the next impact and the joyful reunion of our skins.

"I don't know the odds, Johnny, but it has to be worth trying," Zoey said, a damp sheen on her upper lip as she worked her body, writing in time with my movements.

"So what do I have to do? Just keep doing this?"

"Yes, Johnny. And in as many positions as possible."

"Okay, well..."

Damn it! We've already done every position I know.

"Zoey... um... could you take the lead on that part?"

Zoey reached out for me and I took her hand, relinquishing her knee and certainly not her ass. She squeezed my fingers.

"Don't be embarrassed about experience, baby. I think it's cute, anyways... *oh yes baby yes...* sometimes energy can replace experience. Don't worry about a thing; I'm going to take good care of you."

She pushed me onto my back with the leg she had across my waist, trapping me in some kind of wrestling hold.

"What's this one called?" My cock was twisted away from me, trapped within her and I wasn't sure I was enjoying it.

Zoey continued twisting and eventually wriggled free.

"It wasn't a position, at least I think it wasn't, I was trying to get up."

"Why? I thought we had to try lots of positions?"

"We do, but I got to thinking and remembered there wasn't a bed in the room when the doctor cured me of Ebola."

"Right! Good thinking. So we should try all the positions the doctor did with you?"

"Yes, if I can remember them. I was so scared I was going to die I wasn't thinking straight at the time. But still, I haven't even had a cold since I started practicing tantra."

"Okay, let's do it. What's first?"

Zoey rested her forearms across the back of a chair hand-painted with daisies and roses twining up its legs. She wiggled her ass at me.

"I'm sure the doctor started with this one, sugar."

I decided that the doctor must have been a man of admirable taste. I guided myself too her then took her by the hips urging her against me but she didn't need to be urged and started her hip rolling dance moves again. After only a minute enjoying this new position and an excellent view of her booty, she sat on the chair and took me into her mouth; her lips unlike anything I had ever felt against my cock and it took all my control to slow my breathing and not have it end right there. I'm ashamed to say I had to look away as the sight of her blowing me would have sent me over the edge.

Just as I felt I had it under control, and could dare a quick peek at her lips wrapped around my shaft, she released me, forced me to sit on the chair and then straddled me, rubbing her breasts against my nose and lips, burying my face into them.

"The doctor said that this may have been an important one... oh sugar..."

Zoey would half stand, almost pulling off me, then slide back down to sit in my lap, groaning into my ear. She made sure I teased each nipple one after the other, then standing again faced away from me and backed down into the reverse position. She settled across my lap, placing one of my hands on her breast and guiding the other through the damp thicket between her legs. I flicked the swollen little bulb that flowered there. She squeezed my hand that she had trapped over her nipple, squeezing it until I too squeezed her and then began to moan in time with the flicking of my fingertip on her sex.

She convulsed and I kept rubbing her, biting her shoulder as she came, grinding against my pole and shaking until she pulled my hand away from her pussy and wrapped it around her belly, embracing her.

"Oh that was wonderful, sugar. Simply wonderful... oh..."

Zoey's head slumped forward and I heard whispered breathing.

"Zoey? What do we do now—have we finished?"

"No..." she mumbled, then her ribs rose and fell as she breathed deeper. "Okay... oh wow that was awesome... okay..."

She staggered across the room, swept some old books and some colorful unlit candles off her dressing table, then lay across it, cocking one knee up on its edge and waggling her ass for me. I jumped up, one hand on her ankle and one on her hip and thrust into her again. Zoey moaned, biting into her knuckle, shivering as aftershocks of her orgasm ran through her body. I ran my hand down the curve of her hip, mesmerized by the cocoa satin of her skin, grabbed her shoulder and pulled against her as I ground as deep as I could go. Her hips twitched and I could feel her clamping torturously, wonderfully around me, the cascading pleasure bringing me to the very edge of what I could bear.

"Zoey... uh... I don't think I can last much longer—"

"Then do it—now!"

She pushed powerfully with her hips and I stumbled back. Zoey rolled off the table and knelt in front of me, throwing her hair back over her shoulders, closing her eyes and plumping up her breasts. Oh God she was incredibly sexy.

"All over me, Johnny. The doctor said it was the only way..."

I pulled off the rubber and started to jerk myself off. Zoey reached between my legs, cupping my balls, squeezing them gently in time with my movements. She brought her face so close to me that my tip rubbed against her pillowy lips and at that moment of electric contact I started to spasm lashing her face with a torrent of cum, trailing it over her breasts as I shuddered.

"Oh man," I said. "That was... incredible... my serotonin levels must have been off the chart—"

Zoey's lips parted and she took me in her mouth and I groaned, my eyes closing and my head falling back as she suckled at me.

Faintly in my stupor I heard a lock turning, a few steps and a light rapping at the door.

"Hey Zoey. I saw lights, are still up, girlfriend? Oh dear!"

Still deep within the cotton wool numbness of my subsiding orgasm, I turned my head.

There stood a young blonde woman in a beige raincoat. Beautiful with light makeup; brown eye shadow and pink lips.

It was Gwen Hertzensbrecher.

"Johnny?"

Chapter 14: The Girl of his Dreams

0:21 am

So this was awkward...

My heart pounded and fell on alternating beats. Gwen looked at me, tight lipped with her hands on her hips. I hadn't seen her for over six years and the first time we meet I've got my cock in her roommate's mouth and there's spunk everywhere. There was so much I'd wanted to say to her before the end and I'd thought that I would never get the chance.

"Gwen, wait!"

She slammed the door on her way out.

Zoey's luscious lips slid up my shaft, she pecked a kiss on its tip then she reached for a box of tissues and began to clean herself off.

"That was awkward," Zoey said, dabbing my cum from the side of her nose. "You guys know each other?"

"We did," I said, my voice catching in my throat. "We went to school together."

"Oh, the school you went to with Marcus Goldenrod?"

"Yeah..." I said.

"So wait... you and Gwen and Marcus all went to the same school?"

"Uh-huh."

"Damn it! What a stupid bitch I've been!"

"Huh? What do you mean?"

"Whenever I asked Gwen about her boyfriend she always said it was Marcus Goldenrod. I just, well you know, an elementary teacher dating a trillionaire, I just thought she was teasing me and didn't want to let me know who it really was. We've only been roomies for a couple of months and haven't gotten to know each other that well. Damn, I was wasting my time hunting for him at those parties after all, unless..."

Zoey smiled up at me as she wiped a strand of my man milk from her cleavage.

"Me? Sorry Zoey, I may know Marcus but I'm no trillionaire. I can barely make rent each month."

"Damn. Oh well, at least you're a great fuck."

She got to her feet, rummaged through the piles of clothes on the floor and pulled a thin kaftan out. Her frown softened when she looked at me, shivering in my nakedness, head and shoulders drooped.

"Sugar, what about your sero-whatsit levels? Do you think you're cured?"

I sighed, long and deep.

"You were amazing Zoey. Beautiful, sexy and, wow... sexy as all hell, but I... it's just I..."

"Huh. Poor baby. You like her that much, huh?"

Zoey threw me a pink toweling robe and I slowly pulled it on. She stood in front of me, took both my hands and squeezed them.

"You're a great guy too, Johnny. Funny, sexy and one crazy-ass dancer. You should go and try to talk with her. She's a good listener, tell her the truth, baby. She might even understand. Now scoot, I'm gonna take a shower. The water is funky at night. You might want to give it ten minutes to heat up after me if you're going in."

She swayed her way out the room, leaving the door open and a few moments later I heard the hiss of running water.

I swallowed, looking within myself to find some kind of composure, my fingers tightening into fists. There was no time left, no other chance. I had to do it now.

Gwen leaned against the kitchen bar, staring at an open glossy magazine on the counter and a steaming mug beside it. A faint tendril of steam spiraled up from the kettle's spout. She glanced at me as I came in, then returned to her magazine, flipping to the next page, waiting a moment, then flicking onto the next.

"It suits you," she said.

"What?"

"The robe. Pink suits you."

"Oh. Heh. Yeah. Gwen..."

"Mmm?"

"I wanted to ask you something, can I?"

"Make it quick, Johnny. I've got to get up early tomorrow to catch a plane so I need to be in bed soon."

"You're going away?"

She looked up from her magazine, I searched for a hint of that smile I remembered but there wasn't a trace.

"Marcus and I are going to the Caribbean for a week on his yacht."

I felt empty, too weak to even cry. "Sorry, I forgot you were engaged... congratulations..."

She returned to her magazine, sipping her milky mug between flicking the pages. "We're not engaged... it's not that kind of... who said we were engaged?"

"Marcus did..."

She frowned at me with pursed lips.

"When did he say that?"

"At the party last night."

"He'd had quite a few to drink," Gwen said.

"True... maybe I misheard him."

"Funny, I didn't see you at the party. I was there most of the night."

"Huh? Marcus said you were away on business."

"Business? I'm an elementary school teacher, Johnny. What kind of business trip could I have been on?"

"Oh. I guess I misheard him again. We were standing pretty close to the speakers, it was loud I guess..."

She finished her drink, rinsed the mug and left it in the sink.

"Well, good to see you again, Johnny. I'm going to bed now. Was that all you wanted to ask me?"

"No, wait, Gwen, I wanted to say... I mean I needed to ask... remember when we were kids? Remember when we'd be friends forever? What happened to us?"

She puffed, looked away, then back at me with an angry glare.

"You happened, Johnny. You got to high school and decided to immediately become the world's biggest asshole."

"Wait, what?"

"And I tried, Johnny, I swear I tried. Time and again I'd try to get through to you, to the sweet and funny Johnny that I'd grown up with, but it was useless. You were too much of an asshole to give me an explanation and you'd just brush me off. That and the lying. Eventually I just gave up on you and stopped trying, and I guess you just gave up on yourself too. Classy performance in there with Zoey, by the way. That how you treat all your first dates?"

I felt my face redden and tugged the pink robe tighter around me.

"Gwen, I didn't... I mean... lying? When did I lie?"

"The first day of high school. Obviously trying to impress the older guys, weren't you Johnny? You told everyone you'd had sex with me and I was an easy lay. I was fourteen! Why would you do something like that to me? We were friends, or so I thought."

"Gwen I swear, I never said that. I swear Gwen!"

She crossed her arms over her chest.

"A decade older and still just a lying fourteen-year-old. What hope is there for you if you can't even admit the truth now?"

"Gwen, seriously I never said that—I never would want anything bad to happen to you, I lo—"

"You what?"

"I love you..."

"You don't even know what that means. Is that what you were doing with Zoey? Loving her? You make me sick."

"Gwen, I don't have much time left, there are some things I needed to tell you."

"Get it over with then. Marcus said that you'd been going around telling everyone that I was a slut and about the filthy things you said I'd done with you."

"Marcus?"

"Yes, Marcus. Even your best friend couldn't stand what you'd become."

"And that's why you didn't speak to me?"

"Why would I want to, after you'd been so horrible?"

Something was wrong here. Why would my buddy Marcus say that?"

"Gwen, Marcus told me that you'd told everyone at school that I had a micropenis."

"What? You even can't stop lying now, can you Johnny?"

"Didn't you?"

"Of course I didn't! How would I have known anything about your penis?"

How would she? It didn't make any sense.

"Marcus told me that you'd told everyone I had a micropenis. Then he told you that I'd told everyone that I'd had sex with you. I was picked on and teased every day at high school, and despite it all, I still wanted us to be friends, to be... well who would be interested in a guy with a micropenis?"

She stared at her shoes, simple brown pumps, white socks above them.

"Johnny, I know you had a hard time and didn't have many friends in school, but I really did try to reach out to you. I'm not saying something would have happened, but who knows? All I can say is that I wouldn't have let your penis decide for me whether I liked you or not. That would depend on you."

"Wait, Gwen, are you saying—"

"I'm not saying anything Johnny. It's all in the past and things have changed, I've changed. I just wanted you to know, that if you've been holding a grudge against me all these years, well, I wouldn't have turned you down for a date because of your penis. I'd have turned you down because you were an asshole."

"Oh."

"And you were obviously even lying about the micropenis. I mean, really, I can't believe Zoey actually managed to fit that thing into her mouth."

"Speaking of that Gwen, do you think you could ever—"

"No. we were kids, Johnny. Let's just forget about it."

"But now you know I have a huge—"

"No! You just don't get it, do you Johnny? If I loved you I wouldn't care what you looked like or what other people thought was wrong with you. None of that would matter to me."

"So then—"

"Goodnight, Johnny, and goodbye. I've got a plane to catch and need just a few hours' sleep at the least before I drive over to see Marcus."

"Why doesn't he come pick you up?"

"He's a busy man!"

"Too busy to pick up the girl he intends proposing to?"

"You are an asshole, Johnny. Marcus was the only one who stood by you, no matter how much more of an asshole you became. Now you want to poison that as well? Goodbye, loser."

Gwen walked past me and I heard her door shut. How could loving someone you barely knew hurt so much? I never even got to see her smile before the end.

This was the worst day of my life.

I had wanted one chance with her but I blew it. Just like I'd always blown. Ever since high school. Ever since... that bastard Marcus.

I stared at my fists, wanting to punch him in his arrogant, handsome, trillionaire face. The running water had stopped a minute ago and in the quiet room I could hear a clock ticking. My hands unclenched. This wasn't a movie where the hero chases after the bad guy to exact revenge while his life ticks away. These were the last few hours of my life. I'd failed with Gwen and she hated me. There had to be something worth doing before the end.

Zoey came out the bathroom, her hair pinned up and a towel wrapped around her body. She raised an eyebrow and nodded to Gwen's door. I shook my head and sighed, she gave me a rueful smile, tossed me her damp towel and walked naked back to her room.

The shower was, as Zoey had predicted, lukewarm for a few seconds then ice cold. The frigid torrent cleared my mind and washed the grey weariness from my bones and I felt somewhat bolstered to take on my final hours.

I wandered back to Zoey's room with the towel around my waist and started to pick my clothes out from amongst her mess. She had on a yellow nightshirt with a teddy bear stitched on the front; with no makeup and her hair pulled back she looked much younger than I'd taken her to be when we met at the party.

As I tied my shoes I heard Zoey laugh. She was sitting on the edge of the bed with something in her lap.

"Number Six—Mambo with a foxy African queen! Were you drunk when you wrote this, boy? African queen, really?"

"Yes I was drunk, Very drunk, and a good few years younger too. Are you mad with me?"

She chuckled. "No, sugar. You can call me your queen any time that you like. But do I just get crossed off and then you're on to your next conquest?"

I kissed her on the forehead.

"Zoey, who knows what might happen if I survive the night, but I have a feeling your Ebola magic won't work for me. Take care, sugar," I said.

I shut the door very quietly on my way out.

Chapter 15: I'm Gonna to Phone a Friend

01:03 am

I sat on the cold steps that led up to Zoey's, and Gwen's, brownstone. A supposed night of triumph with the delectable socialite Bianca, the wild Bröstenberg twins, and hippy dreamer Zoey. Wasn't I supposed to be ecstatic? Ah, I was forgetting something:

~~Number 6: Mambo with a foxy African queen~~
~~Number 9: Do it doggy style~~

I looked at the list, waiting for the suffusion of satisfaction it had been providing me each time I'd updated it. I didn't feel smug or even pleased. I felt desiccated; like my heart was just crumbling away. I knew Gwen was only a few meters away, probably sleeping by now. It's a good thing that she never saw The List. I don't think she would be too impressed. My hand rested on my thick thigh, I gave it a little encouraging rub, just to cheer myself up. It was soft and unresponsive. Damn it. Now my magnificent boner had deserted me too. A loser and his flaccid, if impressively large, cock. What a pair we made.

My phone vibrated, I pulled it out and unlocked it. Another close-up photo from Maddie; she'd tied a pink bow through her labial piercings. There was a message attached:

> *I'm lonely, come over and unwrap me!*
> *Maddie xox*
> *Sent from my Aphone.*

I flipped through the other photos. Probably a good thing Gwen hadn't seen my phone either. I paused at one of my new contacts I'd made, hovered my thumb over it and it rang.

"Johnny! How are you getting along?"

"Good and bad, Master."

"Have you upped your game, Johnny? Are you at the next level?"

Bianca, Astrid, Sigrid and Zoey. "Yep. No doubt about that Master. I think you'd be proud."

"I am Johnny. I am. But... there is a trace of sadness in your voice. Not what I'd expect for a man sampling the finest delights the world has to offer. What's troubling you?"

"Have you ever been in love, Master?"

The line went silent and there was a long pause. I wondered if we'd been cut off.

"Are you still there, Master?"

The sigh was that of an old and tired man. Until that moment I would never have thought that a single sigh could convey such remorse, regret and an unfulfilled longing of the soul.

"How many women do you think I've seduced, Johnny?"

"Um, hundreds? Or even thousands?"

"I honestly don't remember. At first I tried to keep track of their names, remember their faces. I kept lists, scrap books, I even wrote notes for my memoirs, but eventually... ah yes, eventually they all start to blur and your memories become hazy and they are lost to time."

"Wow. Not a great way to cheer a guy up."

"What I'm saying Johnny, is that with all those women, never once did I feel what I would call love. Passion, yes. Desire and even joy, yes, but never love. Tell me Johnny, is that your problem? Is that the 'bad' part you are feeling?"

I cradled my head in my hand, my vision blurring as tears began to well up. "Yes Master, it's... she's called Gwen and I..." I trailed off as I tried to gulp down the sobs rising in my throat.

"You love her. Yes, I believe you do. Johnny, listen to me. Not every man who has the talent to be a great pickup artist is destined to become one. If you have a chance, the merest sliver of a chance at love, then go for it, Johnny. Abandon your one final night of passion and throw it all away for love. I wish that I—"

He broke off and I heard muffled gasps. I guess he must have been fighting to control his emotions.

"Master, I... it's no good, it's too late for me. She hates me and there is nothing I can do in the time I have left. I'll just struggle on with this plan and the damned dawn can take me. I don't even care anymore."

The muffled cries on the other end of the line were breaking my heart; despite the pain I already bore I felt enormous guilt at leading him to what must be such a devastating realization.

"Master, I'm so sorry to have put you through this as well... I—"

"Oh yes! OH YES! OH!"

"Master? Are you okay?"

His gasping slowed and I could hear him breathing deeply.

"Sorry Johnny, um, I missed that last part. What were you saying?"

"You missed what I was saying? Master, I was pouring out my heart to you. I thought you were having a breakdown..."

"A breakdown? No, not at all. It's just that, well, Raquel stopped by and she was blowing me just now. Not just licking or teasing me, but going at me like a goddamned Hoover. Johnny, you must know how hard it is to concentrate when she does that swirly thing with her tongue, don't you?"

Asshole. I hung up. I was on my own. He still had the advantage of an admittedly wrinkly and inevitably finite life ahead of him. And me? I had blown any chance of reconciliation with Gwen and had less than five hours to live. What had I been thinking, that she might want someone like me? I was a loser. A jerk. In my last day alive I'd chosen hedonism over love. I was so not worthy of her. I was a totally worthless jackass who'd never amounted to anything, never achieved anything, and—I got it I really did—I just didn't deserve her. Didn't deserve to be happy. May as well just follow this downward spiral into oblivion 'cause I didn't have long to wait for the end.

My thick thigh didn't protrude as much as it used to. I prodded and it was still spongy and soft. Great, now I didn't even have that magnificent erection. What a letdown, facing the end with a floppy.

Chapter 16: The Nightclub

02:42 am

I'd never been to a nightclub and judging by how long I'd spent in the queue so far I was beginning to think I might never. I was completely sober and felt completely out of place waiting in a line outside *The Edge*, what I vaguely knew to be the coolest club in town right now. A muffled bass beat could be heard coming from underground and the buzzing chatter of excited clubbers was the treble. Judging by the crowd this was indeed the place to be, but most of the people queuing were in groups. When they were all girls the giant broad-shouldered security staff simply whistled them through, raising the red cordon as high heels clattered on the iron stairs to the basement, then pressed back on chests as people surged forward.

Groups of guys had a harder time. Some of them simply high-fived the goliath guards and were admitted, but most faced an interrogation; IDs examined, pockets searched. Most were turned away; sometimes I saw the flash of green in a handshake which seemed to be the fastest way through.

I checked my wallet. Just a few dollars left. Do they take credit cards in nightclubs? I hoped they did. I patted my breast pocket then remembered Bianca's roll hitting the counter as I ordered champagne for Astrid and Sigrid. That memory should have cheered me up but it felt like a receding memory; a fading photo. While the experience had been sensational all I was left with was the memory and that alone did not brighten my mood.

"ID."

A hand that a gorilla wouldn't want to shake was thrust at me. I laid my driver's license on his palm with the last of my cash folded on top of it.

Gold teeth glinted under his sneer.

"Dude! Six bucks? Are you fucking kidding me? Get out of here chump."

He swept me out of the line in a single motion, but I grabbed the wrist of his jacket. I had to get in there. There was no more time left.

"Wait. Please. I'm dying, I've got terminal cancer."

His nose twitched and he took a step back.

"Dude, are you serious? Ah, man..."

See? Even this behemoth had a heart. No man could know of my pain and not sympathize with me, no matter how tough or hardened they were. The truth would save me.

I met his gaze and clasped my hands together, desperate to persuade him.

"I've been diagnosed with terminal cancer of the penis. I'm going to die in just a few hours. Please, the last thing I ever want to do is get into this club. Do you think you can find it in your heart to let me in?"

Gorilla-hands' eyebrows knitted and he advanced on me, grabbed me by the shoulders and shook me.

"You think cancer is funny, dude? You think it's some kind of fucking joke? Someone needs to teach you a lesson, asshole, and that someone is—"

"Stop being such a drama bitch!"

Mrs. Robertson slapped the security guy's burly body with her handbag, beating him away from me, his hands raised to ward off the blows.

"Linda, I—"

"Don't Linda me, you big sissy! You should be ashamed of yourself, Maurice. What d'you think your mother would say if I told her I'd seen you behaving like this?"

"But—"

"But nothing! Come on Johnny, you look like you could do with a drink. I know I could."

My jaw flapped but that was the only protest to be heard as Mrs. Robertson dragged me by my hand past the security and down the stairs. The door opened to darkness punctuated by strobing flares and the music erupted around us.

"I love this place! Such youthful energy!"

She had to shout into my ear to be heard, clutching my arm, pressing her breasts against me and her lips brushing my earlobe.

"Mrs. Robertson—" I started to speak but she hugged me tight and the air squeezed from my lungs as I was encased in her plump folds.

"Linda..." I said, and she nibbled my ear and I shivered at the shock of her tongue questing inside. I struggled to break free.

"The bathroom—"

"Together? How naughty, you delicious little boy! We could find an empty cubicle and—"

"No," I croaked. "I really need the bathroom. Please..."

The flesh on her upper arms quivered as she released me and pouted.

"Well, be quick then. I'll get us some drinks and we can start this party! This will be our meeting point in case we get separated. Okay?"

I nodded and let the crowd surround me, the stream of bodies carrying me away.

"Right back here—" Then her voice was gone.

The shocking white of the bathroom lights dazzled me as I stepped in. The room smelled of bleach. I stood blinking for a few moments, shading my eyes as they adjusted. A not particularly convincing transvestite stood in front of a wall urinal, skirt hitched up and whistling as their stream hissed down the drain. Grunts emanated from a closed cubicle; the door vibrated rhythmically.

I splashed water on my face and looked in the mirror. There were dark circles under my eyes and the fluorescent lights had my image bleached to bone with a blue-grey shadow across my jawline and chin. I ran my fingers through my hair, smoothing it back, then dried my hands with a paper towel.

That other Johnny looked back at me, tired and sad. I laid The List beside the basin, scanned it and sighed. Why was I neither proud of my accomplishments nor eager for more?

Gwen.

It was pointless and I was out of time. Why would I even think about her when all I could offer her would be a guy without a cock? No. Stick to the plan, Johnny. You know the pain of living with a micropenis, but having it chopped off totally? Without even the lonely solace of wanking to relieve the frustration? You made the right call this morning, and it's still the right call now. Don't bail on me at the last minute buddy.

I checked my watch. Less than three hours to go. Carpe diem buddy, carpe diem. I grimaced a smile at myself that even I didn't buy. Sighed, forced a tight chuckle, then took a deep breath and headed back into the club.

The bass hits you like a train, the music carrying you with it, but it is the twisting and the pumping of the dancing bodies that drags you onto the floor. There are primitive parts of the brain that respond to the drums, to limbs moving in time with the beats. A tribal energy is in the air, you can smell it as part of the sweat and sex and perfume, and you are powerless to resist.

"Cheer up buddy," the barman said. He was about my age, smiling broadly. "You're supposed to be having fun. What happened to you? Somebody die or something?"

"Not quite yet." I managed a fake grin. "Can I get a martini?"

"Vodka or gin?"

"Vodka, please."

"Coming right up, and while you wait…" He poured an amber inch into a shot glass. "On the house, something to get you in the mood."

Random acts of kindness. How is it that guys who work behind a bar can see into your soul with a glance? I raised the glass to him and knocked it back. Woof. Okay that warmed me up.

My martini arrived and I passed over a credit card.

"You want a tab?" The barman rapped the counter with the edge of the card.

"Sure, I'll be here all night."

He swiped the card and shook his head. "Sorry buddy, declined."

"It's been a busy day. Try these."

The second card got declined too, but the last one worked just fine. It went under the bar somewhere and I was given a black plastic rectangle in return, the logo of the club on one side and "47" in big white numbers on the back. My martini was really strong so I took it easy as I looked around the club. The dance floor was packed, the DJ booth surrounded by speakers. A tall guy with corn-rows and headphones around his neck was up there, shouting to the dancers, and they cheered back at him.

Martini magic did its stuff and after a couple more shots of tequila I was among those bodies, tightly packed, scuffing shoes and sharing sweat. I danced the way that came natural to me, like I did at home in front of the TV. I danced like I did with the Bröstenberg twins, the way Zoey had seen me, and wanted to be with me. Until today I had no idea that I had this special talent, and that women loved it so much. I did my moves, and a chubby brunette in a lacy black dress laughed at me, I presume in delight, pointed at me with both hands and cheered.

I grinned and did a few moves in her direction, she clapped her hands over her mouth, probably to contain her admiration, then with a whoop she started dancing with me. She had friends too, a lean woman in her forties, jeans so low you could see her hip bones, and one with pink hair, a ring piercing her nose and tattoos on her arms. They joined us, giggling when I showed off some bit of improvisation as the music changed to different beats. I caught a glimpse of Mrs. Roberson, perched on a barstool and craning her neck around, scanning the crowd so I slowly gyrated in a semicircle until I had my back to her.

More women came, their boyfriends not seeming to mind. First they glared at me when the girl they were dancing with turned in my direction, then a puzzled frown, then they burst out laughing in amazement at my skillful techniques, shake their heads and release the hand straining to escape them.

I was surrounded by them; cheering at me and waving their arms. The pink-haired one with the tattoos put something in her mouth then caught me by the back of my neck and kissed me. I felt her tongue push past my lips and then a bitter astringent taste. She broke away and handed me a half bottle of water.

"Wash it down," she shouted over the music.

"What was that?" I took a drink, washing away the chemical flavor.

She winked at me. "You know..."

I shook my head. "Know what?"

Pink girl giggled at me. "What do you think? Just something to help the party along."

I stumbled back, stepping on someone's foot then was shoved forward to the pink girl. Was she saying...? Oh damn. I think I've just taken drugs.

"Just relax, go with the flow," Pink said.

It suddenly felt hard to breathe. I started gasping, the press of flesh around me overwhelming and oppressing. I'd never done anything harder than that one reefer I'd tried which had made me puke for over an hour.

Pink stopped dancing and stared at me as I trembled. "You okay?"

"I've never... I mean—"

"Wow, really? I thought you looked the type... well you're in for a great ride—welcome to club land, virgin!"

Pink hugged me, holding on until my chest stopped heaving.

"It's not every day that you lose your virginity. Congratulations!"

"Yeah I know, and thanks, I think..."

"You're going to be fine," she said. "I'll stay with you, and I'm easy to find in the crowd."

Pink tapped her hair, smiled at me and I nodded, the coursing fear giving way a nauseating sick taste in my throat.

"I think I need another drink…"

"What?" Pink cupped her ear and turned her head to me.

"I think I need another drink," I managed a louder voice though my throat just wanted to squeak.

Pink shook her head, took my hands and started dancing again, tugging me along. I shuffled to keep up with her and as I moved I felt the tension ebb away. First and last time for a lot of things today, I guess. It's not like I need to worry about waking up with a monster hangover anyway. So this was how I was going to go out, surrounded by strangers, but that had been most of my life. Who was I going to miss? I never said goodbye to my parents. Never said to Marcus what he deserved. Never said to Gwen…

The music picked up its pace and the crowd cheered as a new DJ took his place, kissing his fingertips and holding them out in a two-armed salute. I cheered with them, feeling the beats through the soles of my shoes. Pink had her arms around the neck of the chubby brunette, kissed her once, hesitantly, then again and they stayed locked like that.

I felt hot, knew my face was flushed, but was helpless in thrall to the music and moving with it, watching the girls make out. The lean woman took my hand, turned me away from them, gyrated in front of me, holding her hair up on the top of her head with both hands, turning her neck to me, looking back to me to see if I was watching. I was. The beat driving my movements were echoed in her twists. Watching her and feeling the music in everything I threw my head back and laughed, giving over to it, surrendering myself. My palms tingled and through them I could feel a magnetic connection linking to an energy that flowed through all of us, joining us and sharing the experience.

Pink and the chubby brunette were back. They made me take my jacket off and the lean woman spoke in my ear, unbuttoning some shirt buttons, placing her hand on my chest. The contact felt amazing, a blessing from a goddess. I didn't know what she said as everything sounded compressed. Everything apart from the music was filtered out. I looked around saw people silently cheering, Pink's lips opened and closed as she danced in front of me. She raised her eyebrows, expecting some response. I smiled and nodded. What did it matter? I felt great.

The chubby brunette patted me on the hips, then on my ass, wriggled out my wallet and placed a slip of pink paper in. Her mouth moved mutely, pointing at the pink slip, putting my wallet back in my pants. I had no idea what she was saying. Why wasn't she dancing?

I felt so free without my jacket, raising my arms, watching the light stream between my fingers. Why hadn't I done this before? It should have been on top of The List. Never mind. Doing it now. I grinned at Pink and she laughed back. Everywhere I turned my head people smiled back at me. A wink from a woman in a yellow T-shirt; a guy who tapped me a one-finger salute; a girl in a black bikini top with kinky black hair and smoldering eyes.

Wow. I kept staring at her, nodding in time with the music. She watched me as she danced, sucking on a lollipop. Her lips were mesmerizing and I felt breathless as they parted around the sticky cherry. Black curls stuck to her damp collar bones and I stared as she teased them away, pink nail varnish the color of her lips. She looked away from me as a guy in a white shirt moved closer to her, leaned over to speak in her ear.

Regret stabbed me stab in the stomach; I sighed and turned back to Pink and her crew. Pink bounced with each step and she called a wordless greeting to me, hugged me around the neck and resumed her bouncing. The DJ started a new track. The piano riff greeted with fists pumping the air, open mouths raised in adulation. I was animated purely by music, closing my eyes, the flashing lights visible through my lids. Each step a note and it flowed through my body.

I opened my eyes and the girl with the bikini top danced in front of me, her hands in the air and her head tilted down. Kinky hair covered her face, so black it shined like metal. She had something tattooed on the insides of her arms in a script I couldn't make out and her skin a light tan with a smattering of freckles. She turned her back to me without looking up, continuing to step to the music, to move her hips and to twist her shoulders. The whiplash shock of the thin black cord the only thing to cover the complete nakedness of her back drew me closer; I wanted to be able to smell her, to feel the heat like glowing mist around her.

Her cowboy boot heels moved a quarter-inch back and I was stuck to that spot on the ground, knowing I should retreat, to give her room to dance, begging for that skin to approach, watching, enraptured by her hips that punctuated their swaying with the kick drum. The heels moved half an inch back again and I smelled her perfume in her hair as she tossed her head to the side, a strand flying across my cheek, a burning line of wet contact that I could feel as her sweat. My hands were either side of her and I felt her warmth, the smell of her suffusing my senses. Giddy delirium so strong I thought my legs might not hold me.

The petals of her arms descended. I pulled back my hands, trembling in retreat and the back of my finger dusted the inside of her arm and was gone. She raised her head, looked over her shoulder at me, thick black eyebrows, hooded eyes, then back to her feet again. She danced on the same spot at the song reached its crescendo, looping, building, ecstatic peak and then burst like the shattering of a blissful note falling all around, and she swayed back, brushing her tight jeans against my crotch.

My hands shook, an inch away from her hips, and she continued to sway as the next track blended in, urging the devoted followers to take up the dance again in a new prayer to music. She rubbed against me and I knew then she did not expect me to step away, that she had chosen to dance there, that she was dancing for me. My heart beating erratically I put my hand on her belt. My thumb hovering like a ghost above her hip, touching, pulling away then with a reckless feeling of elation touching it to her again, stroking as we moved our hips together.

Her head rolled back, resting on my shoulder. That kinky black hair across my face, drowning in the French musk of her perfume and her damp heat. My forefinger moved from the belt, cautiously creeping then joined my fortunate thumb on her hip swell. I felt her sigh as my chest touched her back, speckled with perspiration, the heat of our skins feeling beyond normal contact. She reached up, clasping my head, leaning it to hers and she kissed me on the neck; the shock running through my spine and a twitch from inside my pants.

Emboldened I moved my hand across her belly, the slightest swell of softness over lean dancer's muscle, and she arched her back forcing her flesh against my palm. Her shoulders against my chest and her ass against my groin. I gasped at the contact, feeling her whole body in one movement after such lingering, tantalizing teasing. I tried to turn her around but her grip on my head tightened and she held me locked there. Rubbing herself against me as the bassline rumbled and the world became a pulsing, burning, spinning plateau of our melding skin, sticky and slick at the same time, filled with electricity.

Reaching fever pitch the tune reverberated through its final loops and the strobes flooded the room in absolute white. Everyone's arms in the air, hers rising with them. My hands stroking from her shoulders to her wrists then she twined her fingers into mine and we became a spotlight statue.

The music died away, thunderous applause for the outgoing DJ, rapturous screams for his successor. She turned around, dragging herself against me, looked up, smiled sleepily and thumbed toward a darker corner, back from the speakers and the dance floor.

I followed her, clarity growing in my senses as the fog cleared by degrees. She lounged on a stackable plastic chair, her legs spread and the toes of her cowboy boots pointing at the ceiling. She twirled her lipstick-slicked lollipop between lips that tickled with a smile. I sat down beside her, feeling the temperature lower from just being away from all those bodies, and noticing for the first time how much my feet throbbed. How long had we been dancing for?

She bobbed the lollipop at me. "Cool," she said, a thick accent.

"Me?" I tapped my chest.

"Da. Cool."

The lollipop went back in her mouth. I'd never thought it would be possible to be jealous of candy.

"I'm Johnny Johnson, please to meet you. You're one hell of a dancer."

She shook the lollipop from side to side.

"Nyet. No English."

I was going to go with Russian as the accent. That little smile still toyed with the edge of her mouth. Her grey-blue eyes were fringed with thickly mascaraed lashes and a thin strip of pale blue eye shadow. Raised in a culture where I'd been bombarded with images of beautiful women since childhood I think we reached a stage when that symmetry and perfection becomes bland, and from overstimulation we slowly stop reacting to it. This girl tore up all the glossy posters, smashed the movie screens and completely redefined what it could possibly mean to be beautiful. Sitting this close to her I had to remind myself to take each breath, each time. Not daring to take my eyes off her in case she was a drug fueled dream that would wisp away as my narcotic euphoria faded.

I thumbed my chest. "Johnny," I said. "Johnny."

I pointed at her with an encouraging smile. She ran the lollipop across her lips and nodded.

"Natasha," she said.

Natasha held out her hand, I took it and kissed it and she burst out laughing, her white teeth flashing as she chattered some Russian.

"You're so beautiful; you don't understand a word I'm saying, but thank you. The last thing I see in this world will be you, and I'll go without regrets, so thank you."

I did have regrets, and was trying to put them out of my mind. I shook my head as if I could shake those thoughts loose and forget about them. I grinned at Natasha, observing me from behind the sexily demure shield of her lollipop. She shrugged, bemused I guess, but returned my smile.

There was no point in trying to sit here and talk if we couldn't communicate. I stood, still holding her hand.

"Do you want to dance some more?"

I waved at the writhing bodies and wriggled my hips. Natasha got up, glanced to the dance floor and shook her head.

"Nyet."

"Oh."

Most of my euphoria faded away. So this was it. Over so soon, just a few dances then we would be strangers again.

She tugged on my fingers, twirled the stem of her lollipop, and led me away, around the less packed edge of the room. Mrs. Robertson had her arms around the neck of a bodybuilder wearing a tight T-shirt and very thick glasses. I shaded my face with one hand as we slipped past. At the coat check booth Natasha handed over a pink piece of paper and an older guy with tired eyes went through a rack of coats and jackets, returning with a grey woolen wrap which she slung around her shoulders, tying it at the side. I had a vague recollection, looked in my wallet and was surprised to find a receipt of my own, handed it over and recognized my jacket when he gave it to me.

Natasha took my hand and walked me out the club, up the stairs and into the street. The cold bit straight into my damp skin. I turned my collar up and marveled at the scantily-clad girls relaxing unperturbed against the wall by the club entrance, sharing a cigarette. None of them could hold a candle to Natasha.

She pulled me along gently. The absence of music had left a gaping hole in my senses, the monochrome streets and only the distant sounds of sporadic traffic. I stumbled after her, my legs heavy and dull, trying to remember how I'd got here. If she hadn't been guiding me I think I'd have just lain down and slept by the curb.

We crossed the street, long yellow lights washing over us as a car passed, then cutting through a dark alley to another street, and up some stairs. Natasha unlocked a door then we were inside a half-lit foyer, waiting for an elevator to arrive.

Natasha's hand crept around the back of my neck, drew me to her and her eyelashes fluttered down. Her lips brushed mine, lightly. She pulled back, then kissed me harder and I could taste her sticky sweet cherry smell, that French musk in her hair.

The elevator pinged, doors whining open and the light inside spilling out, too bright for me but Natasha dragged me in, pushed me against the mirrored wall and kissed me again. Over her shoulder I watched her stroking me, groping me, writhing against me. The voyeuristic pleasure reached my mind before the physical sensations did; my tiredness melted away as I felt her lips on my neck and on my collar bone as my heart beat faster.

Another ping and she released me. I looked from the image of her in the glass to the sultry, seductive woman in front of me. Natasha crossed the hall, unlocked a door and stepped inside. A light came on casting a rectangle of white across the hall floor. I followed her, stood at the doorway and leaned against the door frame, one hand on each side.

It was a small room, cooker on one side, TV on the other, between them a single bed with white sheets and two pillows. She shrugged off her woolen wrap, dropped it on the foot of the bed. I breathed in sharply at the sight of her almost completely naked back, remembering the rush of breathlessness she'd caused me at the club. How long ago was it? It felt like hours, or a different life.

Natasha turned to face me, still sucking that lucky, lucky candy. Her hands went up, behind her hair, worked a moment, then came back with the top strings to her bikini. She cradled her breasts in her hands, still covered by the triangles of black fabric. The strings fell down and a further inch of flesh was uncovered.

"You're incredible," I said.

It didn't matter to me that she didn't understand; I needed to say it aloud. The utterly perfect symmetry of her eyes held me captive. My mind was clear and calm. I knew she was the most incredible looking woman I had ever seen, or would ever see again. She crossed her arm across her breasts, covering them as the cloth slipped a bit more. Natasha's other arm reached behind her, tugged, and the strings at the side fell loose.

Waiting like that, holding my breath the faces of Dr. Yu, Kristen, Raquel, Madison, Victoria, Bianca, Astrid, Sigrid and Zoey went through my mind. From crazy to cute they had everything, but there was another face there, with a smile so wonderful that it became the most important thing in the world.

She dropped the bikini and beckoned me in. No man could resist that image, moving her hips to a slow dance only she could hear, and I felt myself rising, hardening in an uncontrollable biological response.

My feet hadn't moved. Why wasn't I slamming the door behind me and jumping on her? I had no doubt that she was at this very moment, the hottest girl on the planet. I knew then this was just biology. It wasn't what I needed, what I wanted. It wasn't love.

"I'm sorry," I said, and shook my head, straightening up and letting go of the door frame. I took a step back.

Natasha stopped dancing, tilted her head as she examined me.

"Johnny?"

I shook my head again.

"I'm sorry, Natasha... Nyet..."

I turned and left, hitting the elevator button. Her voice came through the doorway, harsh and shrill. I didn't really need to be able to speak Russian to understand that she probably wasn't saying nice things about me. As the elevator doors closed behind my back I heard a final curse and the door slam.

I was sorry if I'd hurt her feelings, or even if I'd just left her sexually frustrated, but there was something I needed to do. I checked my watch.

04:50 am

Damn it. Nearly out of time. I've only got a couple of hours left. Yesterday morning when Dr. Felicia Yu broke the terrible news to me it didn't take all that long for me to come to my decision, though I admit her sudden interest in me may have tipped the scales a bit. It seemed too simple then, that even having lived a virgin with a micropenis my whole life, there was that tiniest sliver of hope that remained that one day I'd get my chance to be happy. And that last remnant of hope would be gone forever if they chopped off my cock completely. Fairly simple alternative then, to make the most of the very little time that remained until the disease took me and I died. Think with your cock, Johnny, not with your heart. I had no intention of going back to Dr. Yu and getting 'cured'. I never did.

Until now.

You see the crazy part of me that had clung to a desperate hope, growing fainter as the years passed, believing that one day I would be happy, had been brutally silenced when Dr. Yu made her prognosis. How that part of me had managed to survive, crushed and charred and trampled by disappointment, failure and rejection, I don't know, but in a moment of introspection I saw within the pulverized blackened ashes of my soul, a single spark of light. A tiny diamond of a hope that could never be broken.

And I knew what that hope was.

Chapter 17: Chasing the Girl of his Dreams

04:53 am

A little light traffic went sporadically down the street, people going to open up shops and cafes. Waking up the city one neon strip light after the other. A dump truck rumbled past, its tinny radio piping a poppy trail. I looked for street names, jogged around a corner and checked again. I didn't really know this neighborhood. Where was I? Should have been paying more attention when Bianca drove us to the party but my terror had seen to that. The Porsche! Kristen will kill me if something has happened to it. Oh wait. Probably don't need to worry about that after all. I patted my pocket. At least I'd managed to hang onto my wallet.

Spots of rain began to fall and I got my phone out. Maybe I could get a GPS signal? Damn. Stupid thing was on its last flashing amber bar of battery. There were six more messages from Madison. I swiped to get my maps up but rain drops smeared the screen and a video from Maddie started up.

Whoa—that was a really close-up shot of her—then the screen went black. Typical. Stupid thing barely lasted a day any more. I took the battery out, with trepidation licked the terminal like they do in spy thrillers, stuck it back in. No use, just a stupid little red light that lit up for a moment then faded hopelessly away.

My arms hung by my sides and the rain started coming down in earnest, plastering my hair to my face, running down my neck and under my collar. So much for final chance. I was going to die alone and lost, in a city that I'd spent the last few years trying to be as lost and alone as I could manage to make my existence.

I crossed the street, jogged down it, around another corner, looking at storefronts and billboards, searching for something familiar. The brownstones gave way to large houses, set back from the street by green front yards. On the hill behind them, rising in grey silhouette to the pre-dawn light, were the mansions of the stars and the business elite.

There was no point. I had no idea where I was going. I couldn't find my way back to Zoey's house, or even know if Gwen was still there. I banged my head against the slick Plexiglas windshield of an empty bus stop. There was a framed timetable and yellow sign for a coach tour of *Houses of the Stars!*

A bus pulled up and I stepped in, maybe I could get to the airport before it was too late! I fumbled in empty pockets that didn't hold even a dime, pulled out my thin wallet and saw two cards that I knew had already been maxed out, and the black plastic tab counter from

The Edge where my last card should be.

I lurched out the bus and slumped onto the slatted grey grille of the bench, my legs a dead weight and without the spirit to go on. The hydraulics of the bus doors whistled and it pulled away.

The yellow coach tour sign had a map of the neighborhood with a route marked in red. It was punctuated by little gold stars that were numbered and a legend down the side identified the residence of each paragon of success. I read the list of names with revulsion for anyone who had ever been happy in their life.

1. Has-been.

2. Has-been.

3. Hated your last record.

4. Hated your last movie.

5. I hate all of you in your smug happy lives.

6. Hate—oh yes. A special hate, a loathing for you, Mr. Marcus Goddamn Perfect Goldenrod.

Damn you Marcus. You even denied me the chance to say goodbye to her. I didn't think it was going to happen, I thought I could keep it steady until the end, but the desperate unfairness of it all coiled in my stomach, gripped at my throat. I took a couple of ragged gasps, tears blurred my vision and then I started to cry, my shoulders shaking as I sobbed. I wailed at a pitch you should never hear from a grown man and that breaks your heart when you do.

It was all so futile. Why I'd even bothered to keep trying, why I'd picked myself up after surviving the fall that ended up killing Mrs. Podenski. Why I'd lived my quiet life alone after moving to the city. Why I thought one final, fantastic day of getting everything I'd always wanted would have somehow made it all right in the end.

Between heaving bawls I got out The List. This was supposed to make it worth it, that you lived your life achieving dreams, and that somehow it would make it easier at the end. I scrunched it up, raised my hand to toss it into the street, paused to say goodbye to it all, even if I was the only person to hear.

It demanded a farewell.

I spread The List out on my knee. Read it over one more time, then realized that it was trying to tell me something, something I'd written in plain sight but never understood until now. I stood, wiping my snotty, bleary face with my pocket square and The List went back in my jacket.

My steps were firm, steady, getting faster. I started to jog, my teeth gritted, my arms pumping and breaking into a run. The rain drenched me, refreshed and awakened me and I sprinted at top speed up the gently sloping sidewalk, past the houses that grew in size as they retreated from view behind tall walls and security gates.

I skidded to a halt, panting deeply but my fists still tightly balled. I stalked up the drive, wide enough to take two Hummers side by side. The double security gates were open and on the wall where the house number should be was a silver and mirror plaque with a stylized capital A.

As I approached the gate two very smartly dressed guys in dark suits approached from either side. Despite the poor light they wore sunglasses.

"Sir, this is a private residence. Please return to the street."

He undid the single button on his suit jacket and slipped his hand inside.

"It's okay. I'm a friend of Marcus," I said. "I just wanted to wish him a nice holiday."

Behind the security guards two white lights flared, blinding me. There was the soft purr of a very powerful but discreet engine.

"Johnny! What are you doing here, champ?"

Marcus leaned out the window of a very long and wide silver car, made a dismissive gesture with one finger and the guards both melted away.

All I wanted to do as I looked at his handsome smiling face was to wrap both hands around his throat and squeeze. Squeeze and not let go as he went redder and redder and his eyes bulged and his lips went blue.

"Just passing through, old buddy. Wanted to say bye to you guys before you flew out. Is Gwen here?"

Marcus darted a glance past me, then back to my face.

"Sorry, champ. You always seem to miss her. She's already at the airport, I'm kinda running late myself, so—"

"Wait, she said she was going to your place as soon as she woke up. She said you were too busy to—"

"I don't know what to say Johnny, but I really need to get going. If you could just step away from the car..."

My shoulders sagged. That was my last chance. He raised an open palm to me, leaned back in his chair and the shadows covered his face. His car started to move forward, but suddenly it stopped. Two squeaky honks came from behind me and through the open window I heard Marcus sigh.

I turned to see Gwen pulling up by the curb in an old blue Volkswagen, and she waved through her side window. Behind her, framed by the outlines of the high-rises and skyscrapers of the city, an orange glow worked its way up the sky.

Chapter 18: Johnny Johnson Vs. The World

05:59 am

"I thought you said she was already at the airport, old buddy." My voice was tight. I tried to keep it level because if I didn't, well, I felt like my last living act may be to murder someone with my bare hands.

"Johnny, I–"

Marcus' car roared forward, leaving me in a cloud of exhaust fumes and acrid scorched rubber. I started after him pounding my feet against the tarmac, but he had already reached his destination after I had only taken a few steps. His tires shrieked as he spun the car around, half blocking the street but lined up for a speedy exit.

"Gwen, now!" He was half out the car, reaching for her and I saw her head flick from Marcus to me, frowning as she struggled to work out what was going on.

The milk tanker truck came from nowhere. I heard the air horn, looked up as it swerved to avoid Marcus' car, steam jetted up between the wheels as the driver fought not to let the vehicle jack-knife. He must have seen Gwen's Volkswagen too late. I saw him let go of the steering wheel, shielding his face with his arms as the cab ploughed into her.

The Volkswagen flipped over onto the perfect lawn that led up to the walls of the Goldenrod estate, and crashed into the ground. The impact side was crushed half through, the windshield fractured, hanging half open as a stiff opaque sheet.

I could distantly hear myself screaming her name as I started running for her. Horror nearly managed to paralyze me as flames licked out from under the buckled bonnet. Marcus was already there, pulling at the windshield, fighting to get it clear. We tore it away together and both saw her trapped in there, blood running down her temple and cheek where she had smacked her head, buried beneath the airbag and the twisted passenger seat which had been driven into hers.

She blinked; half closed eyes and her lips moved.

"What happened...?"

"Gwen darling, are you alright?" Marcus shouldered me out the way, reaching inside and pulling at the seat belt. "Can you reach the catch? We have to get you out of here."

The truck driver screamed for us to get to safety. I wrenched myself away from Gwen to see what the problem was. My spine spasmed as I saw the fire rising up the front of his cab. Behind it a black tear in the side of his tank and his cargo gushed out, the pool spreading and moving toward us. The driver ran away down the street, waving his arms, shouting for everyone to get clear of the blast.

"We've got to get her out of there now!" I yelled.

My turn to push past Marcus, to tug just as pointlessly at her belt. Gwen's eyes fluttered open.

"Johnny? What... are you doing... here?"

"It's okay, Gwen, just lie steady. We're going to get you out of here. Marcus, help me move this seat... Marcus?"

I twisted around to see Marcus backing away from the wreck, the flames of the Volkswagen that had now climbed up through the wheel arch, charring the tire and sending a stinking spiral of black into the sky. His gaze flicking from the car to widening pool; just a few meters away.

"I... there's nothing we can do..." He had the back of his hand against his mouth, pale face as he looked past me to Gwen, then with a sob he backed away.

"Marcus, you bastard! We need your help! Get back here!" My throat was raw with the fumes and my yelling didn't stop him staggering to safety—wild eyes staring at us.

"Johnny... has Marcus...?"

"Don't worry about him, Gwen. Save your strength, I'll get you out of there."

She nodded and I reached further inside, ground glass grating against my jacket. I struggled to reach the belt clasp.

"Gwen, do you think you can release it?"

She forced her arms free of the airbag which was slowly deflating, and grabbed the lock with both hands and shook it.

"It's stuck; the chair is buckled into it..." Her eyes widened as she looked over my shoulder at the leaping frames. "Oh God, I'm going to die—"

"Shut up, Gwen! You're not going to die! If only I could just..."

The steering column had become dislocated in the crash and I had to crawl further in through the vacant window, my arm twisting past the steering wheel. I got my fingertips onto the lock clasp, but the metal tab had been twisted against the lock and the frame of the passenger seat crookedly compressed against it.

"Johnny..."

"Almost got it..."

"Johnny... you have to go... the fire..."

"I'm not going anywhere without you, Gwen. Nearly—"

My forefinger and thumb closed about the bent tab; the toughest, most resilient alloy ever created by the German auto industry to ensure your safety. I tightened my grip. Muscles leapt into life down my disproportionately well-defined right forearm.

The heat of the flames at my back. The shadows cast across Gwen's face dancing in my peripheral vision. Focus. Tense. Squeeze.

"Johnny! Save yourself!" Gwen pushed on my shoulder, trying to force me out of the car.

"Not without you, Gwen." My teeth ground together as cords twisted down my arm, the pressure building in my pincer grip.

"It's too late, Johnny! I'm not worth dying for!"

"You're worth everything in the world, Gwen."

Sweat trickled into my eyes and my grimace became the fiercest grin. I knew right then why I'd been born like I was, what I'd been born to do, and before my last hour ticked past I would do it. Each day of torment, desperation and loneliness had been leading up to the moment when I, and only me on the whole goddamn planet, could save the life of Gwen Hertzensbrecher.

The full awful force of my micropenis masturbation grip tore the metal tab apart, the plastic housing a moment's afterthought to wrench loose, then her belt came free.

"Johnny!"

I wriggled back, pulling her with me, clambering through the shattered windshield opening and helping her to her feet.

She clung to me. "Johnny…"

The pool reached us, a bolt of fear speared through me as it lapped against the car. My arm wrapped around her waist, lifting her off her feet, my legs pumping as I drove us forward.

The explosion hurled us across the lawn, a second later even louder double explosions as the cab and then the tank incinerated themselves. Echoes pulsed distantly in deafened ears.

My breathing slowed. I lay on top of Gwen, my clothes singed and smoking, my legs soaked with spilled milk. Her face smudged with blood and soot, and her eyes closed.

"Gwen, are you okay?"

I brushed away a blond strand from her eyes. They opened slowly and I saw once again that smile that made everything else pale into nothingness. The smile that was worth more to me that the whole world, than my life, than anything. Dimly I heard Marcus crying out for help but if Gwen heard him she gave no sign.

"Johnny... you saved me. But why risk your life for me?"

I laughed, even though my eyes brimmed with tears.

"I couldn't live without you, Gwen Hertzensbrecher."

"Oh, Johnny, but you said—"

I kissed her as dawn broke. It may have been ungentlemanly of me to take the rescued maiden's reward without actually being offered it, but time was running short, and besides, I'd recently learned that girls like self-confidence, and I had quite a helping of.

Gwen's lips melted beneath mine like warm ice cream sundae and I held her and she held me right back. With a sigh from both of us our lips parted.

"Johnny, all these years... what happened to you?"

So I told her, as much as I had pieced together. The truth about my micropenis. That Marcus, my best buddy, had spread the story so that she would not be interested in me, but panicking when she showed little reaction, lied to her that I had told everyone that I'd slept with her and that she was a slut. When you're in high school there are so many truths that you never question, even if most of them are only lies, rumors, urban myths or gossip.

I'd believed them, she'd believed them, and in the end Marcus won.

"No," she said, shaking her head slowly, smiling dreamily at me. "He hasn't won, Johnny. I always felt something for you, and it confused and haunted me. We have a chance now. We can start again. Find out what would have happened if Marcus hadn't interfered and things had happened as they should have."

I looked away from her, stifled a gasp, and steadied my nerve.

"Gwen, we might not have that chance."

As I looked back to Gwen her perfect, heart-lifting smile faded, bemusement taking its place.

"What do you mean, Johnny?" She touched my cheek with a fingertip, traced my lips as she rolled hers together, savoring the memory of our first kiss.

"Gwen, I..." I sat up, pulled her up and held her hands between us. "I told you about my micropenis, and am delirious that it doesn't bother you. I guess so many things in my life would have been different if I'd know that ten years ago, but that's past now. The thing is, I woke up yesterday with an enormous erection. I was so happy I thought I'd been given a second chance at life, but the doctor... the doctor told me it was cancer, and that I only had a day to live. Gwen, I... I decided that I'd rather not live, and that I'd spend this as my last day alive. That's why you found me with Zoey and... and Gwen, there were others. Many others..."

"Johnny," she said with a tear on each cheek. "It's so cruel, isn't there something they can do?"

I gasped, struggling with the words. "Complete amputation of my penis. It's the only thing they can do."

Gwen hugged me, holding my shaking body in her arms as I cried against her shoulder. Warm, yielding, the scent of her, alluring, exciting. My cries faded away as I felt the desire throb in me. She turned my face to hers, parted her lips and kissed me. My erection grew harder, thicker and I felt an odd wooziness, like the edge of sleep when you can still clutch the fading strands of your dream.

My head felt light, a different part of me yet so heavy I couldn't keep it up. I collapsed, the pale morning light fading to black in my vision. Gwen's voice so faint and coming from far away, and it was the last thing I could hear.

"Somebody phone an ambulance! Please!"

Chapter 19: Johnny Climaxes

The lights were too bright. I raised my hand to shield my eyes. Was this heaven? The afterlife? My head throbbed, my mouth was parched and I couldn't feel my legs. Great. I'd arrived at heaven with a hangover.

"Mr. Johnson?"

A muffled voice, off to the side. I moved my lips but couldn't form words. My throat was so dry.

"Mr. Johnson? Are you awake? How are you feeling?"

A paper cup touched my lips, cold water trickling into my mouth, running down my chin. A tissue wiped me and the cup returned. I managed to swallow some of it. The brightness receded somewhat. I cracked open my eyes.

"Dr. Yu?"

"Welcome back, Mr. Johnson. You gave us quite a scare there for a while. We nearly lost you."

My heart skipped a beat, I tried to claw back my sheets, my arm moving sluggishly and trailing an intravenous drip tube. Felicia held me down with little effort.

"Settle down, Mr. Johnson. Everything is fine. There's nothing to worry about."

"But... my cock?"

"We didn't need to operate after all. Your cancer has gone into remission of its own accord."

"What!"

"Quite so. Your serotonin levels must have been extremely high. I've never had a case of spontaneous remission in a tumor so advanced. Positive thinking can only do so much, regardless of what those sensationalist 'I beat cancer through the power of positive thinking' books say. Nonetheless, here you are."

I didn't know how to feel, happy I should be, elated even, but the shock at being alive, and also the prescription-grade meds they had me on left me confused. I recognized this buzz. These were the meds they had me on after my suicide attempt. Why were they dosing me with them now?

"Felicia... Dr. Yu, are you sedating me?"

She looked up from her clipboard and over the top of her glasses at me.

"Mr. Johnson, not everything has worked in your favor."

"What do you mean, doc?"

"The tumor is gone, Mr. Johnson."

"And I'm healthy, right?"

"Yes, Mr. Johnson, but without the tumor you are back to having a micropenis again."

I slumped against the pillow. I'd never thought about this, never thought I'd have to go back to... I raised my right hand, gazed at my powerfully muscled forefinger and thumb.

"No... It can't be..."

Dr. Yu chuckled, laid my chart on the bed and smiled at me.

"Just my little joke, Mr. Johnson. I like fucking with patients when they're on meds. They're considered too unreliable as witnesses and so are never able to submit formal complaints."

"Huh? I don't—"

"It's okay, Johnny. They tumor is gone, but it stretched your penis out to a pretty enormous size. With arousal you'll be able to fill it and use it as you were. You just need to be careful of your blood pressure as you learn. We can't have you passing out every time you get an erection, can we?"

"No," I said, realizing that I was slightly scared of her.

"Now," Felicia said, leaning over the bed and sliding her hand under the sheet. "Do you need a medical opinion to check everything is in working order?"

My knees jerked to the side and I held down the sheets against them.

"I'm fine!" My voice was a little squeaky, but she withdrew her hand anyway.

"If you say so. Now, you have a visitor."

Dr. Yu opened the door and Gwen rushed in, threw herself across my chest and showered my cheeks and forehead with kisses.

"Johnny, you're alright! I was so worried, at one point the doctors said they didn't think you had the strength to pull through." Her eyes were puffy and bloodshot and she wiped away a sniffle and slowly the radiant sun of her smile dawned on me.

"I guess I had something to live for after all, Gwen."

Gwen looked at a crumpled piece of paper in her hand.

"Dr. Yu, can you give us a few minutes alone, please?"

"Okay, but don't over-excite him. He's been through a lot and needs to recover his strength. I'll be back in a few minutes, I have another patient next door who I need to break some rather bad news to."

I heard the door close and we were alone.

"Gwen—"

"Johnny, wait. There is something I need to ask you. I found this in your jacket when we were in the ambulance on our way here. You were completely unconscious, the paramedics said your blood pressure was dangerously low, that you were slipping into a coma. I didn't know if there was someone we needed to call. I... I found this note..."

She spread out The List, held it up for me to see. Her hands were trembling.

"Johnny, is it true? Is this—"

"Gwen, I can explain! I'd been so lonely; can't you imagine what it's been like for me all these years? I swear to you; I made that list when I was very drunk and lonely, and then finding out that I only

had twenty-four hours to live, well, I decided to attempt to do it. I'm sorry if you feel betrayed but—"

"Is this true? Is this the most important thing you wanted to do before you died?"

Gwen's finger was at the top of the list. The first thing I'd written after listening to the motivational speaker. I remember staring at it for a long time after I'd written it. Realizing then that it would never come true, resigning myself to that and slowly working my way through a list of things that seemed even vaguely attainable.

Number 1: Make things right with Gwen Hertzensbrecher

"Gwen, I didn't think I'd ever see you again."

She squeezed me tight, pressing her cheek against mine and I suddenly understood I wasn't in trouble.

"Oh Johnny, it's the most romantic thing I've ever heard of. You loved me even though you thought I'd destroyed your life. You poor, sweet, lovely thing—"

"Ahem," said Dr. Yu, standing in the doorway, averting her gaze from us and pretending to check her clipboard.

"What's up, doc?" I said, unable to control my wide grin as Gwen nuzzled into me.

Through the wall from the next room I heard a banshee wailing; endlessly shrill and inhuman.

"Your poor friend Mr. Goldenrod had his penis blown off in the tanker explosion. We've fitted him with a silicone prosthetic but he's having a hard time adjusting to the change."

I wasn't sure how I felt when I heard about Marcus, but quickly realized that with Gwen by my side I simply didn't care anymore.

"Poor guy. What about me, Dr. Yu?"

"Your test results came back fine, Mr. Johnson. Just fine. Gwen, I'm going to need you to take special care of him. Regular but varied sexual intercourse, no less than three times a day. We must keep those serotonin levels as high as possible to ensure the remission. Can you manage that?"

Gwen smiled; the smile I had always been in love with even when I didn't know, celestially beautiful and adorable.

"I don't think that's going to be a problem, Dr. Yu. We've got so many lost years to make up for. I never saw Marcus for what he really was and, well to be honest, there are a whole load of things left on Johnny's list that I want to try myself."

"Gwen!"

"Hush, Johnny, you need to keep your strength up. All you need to do now is kiss me."

And then she kissed me.

The End

Epilogue

I wriggled my toes against the setting sun, stretched out on the canvas lounger, enjoying the lapping of the waves against the golden beach and the soothing strains of Hawaiian music drifting over from the bar. The shoeless waiter delivered our ice-filled orange cocktails—Sex on the Beach, naturally. Gwen and I clinked glasses and settled back to sip them.

"Your guests have started arriving, Mr. Johnson."

"Thanks, Davis," I said to my waiter. "Keep them by the main pool area. Gwen and I will be up to join them when we've finished watching the sunset."

"Very good, Mr. Johnson." Davis padded softly away.

We watched the blues darken, the orange disk swell, shimmering as it began to touch the horizon, melting into its own reflection.

"It's so beautiful, Johnny. I just love it here," said Gwen, reaching from her lounger to twine fingers with me.

"It's a magical place, my love," I said. "I'm so glad you bought it. Probably our favorite pad."

In the wild, heady days following my release from the hospital,

Gwen and I had gone through the crazy intoxication of falling in love, more and more each day. The sex, well the sex was awesome, but I'd had no idea how much more wonderful it could be when you were with someone you loved and who loved you right back.

I got brought back down to earth with the call from Kristen, wanting to know where the hell her car was, then by a series of rather unpleasant gentlemen who represented the credit cards that I'd maxed out. Dodging repo men and living on the run with Gwen wasn't what I had in mind until a call from Bianca changed everything.

Two days later I was sitting on a couch next to Oprah, telling my story—well a PG-rated version of it anyway. That evening I had a call from the president of Massive Wang Condoms Inc. who wanted me to be the face—and schlong—of their organization. He made me an offer which, after getting my voice back, I reluctantly accepted.

Things just got better every day, and my celebrity status took me to the pinnacle of the career of stardom; reality TV shows, of course. Finally I took time to write down my memories of the whole crazy ride, this book you're reading right now, in fact. That pretty much brings us up to date, dear reader, watching the sun set over my private beach with the love of my life, Gwen Hertzensbrecher, by my side.

And what have I learned from it all? Just that sometimes when you think you've had a raw deal you might just find you've been dealt the hand that you really needed after all.

Just like me.

Some time later, somewhere else.

Darkness. Cool, still air. The deep stillness of being hundreds of meters below ground. Just on the edges of peripheral vision red lights winked slowly. The hiss and wheeze of an artificial respirator. The deeply reassuring smell of antiseptic.

INITIATE

Boot sequence complete.

Project mega prosthesis initiate...

Power levels... Check

Hydraulic pressure... Check

«Awesome Computers» AI boot sequence... Complete

Clustered around the aluminum-framed bed, the white-coated scientists nervously checked clipboards, tapped gauges, frowned at bouncing white dots on glowing monitor screens. On the bed, the figure stirred; groggy at first as the haze of tranquilizers fades away.

He sat up, scowled, and tore the drip feed tube from his forearm. Ripped off the sticky sensor pads on his temples. He looked down to his lap, covered by a thin sheet of fabric. Beneath the fabric something stirred. Something inhuman and unnatural. Something monstrous.

Marcus chuckled, his voice rising in pitch as his head lolled back and he roared at the ceiling.

"It took a billion dollars... every penny I had... but it'll be worth it, oh yes, it'll be worth it."

The camera zooms in to a tight shot of his crazy, darting eyes.

"I'm coming for you Johnny. I will have my revenge..."

Johnny will return, in...
Johnny Johnson 2: Marcus' Revenge
aka Machine vs. Melanoma

Before You Go!

I hope you enjoyed this book and are fired up by a burning desire to shout the author's name from any conveniently located rooftop. Emerging authors are deeply grateful for each and every reader they connect with. It would mean the world to me if you took a few moments to click/tap/poke your review online.

Thank you, and see you soon!

JJ

Also by Vincto Publishing

The Jewel of Nineveh

A Craft of Shadows Book
Diavosh Bassiti

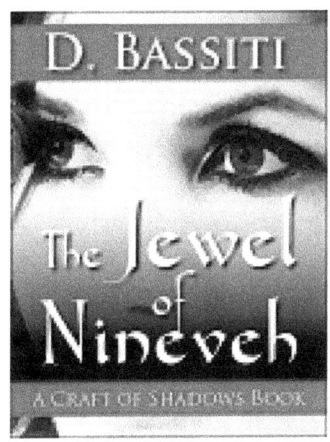

A lone thief fleeing conflict is trapped in a city being torn apart by
intrigue, and finds his talents gain him the unwelcome attention of
vying factions. His endurance and cunning are tested to breaking
point as he struggles to stay alive and the spectre of war descends. As
the stakes grow higher than his own problems he faces a dilemma; can
one man make a difference?
—"A richly woven Persian rug of a story".

God of Thieves: Initiation

A Craft of Shadows Book
Diavosh Bassiti

Divided by generations of hatred, an ancient city faces a barbarian invasion that will destroy them all. A feral orphan forced to kill and steal just to survive, manipulated by those he trusts. And at the center of everything, a master thief spins a web of treachery and deception as he is slowly consumed by madness.
Sometimes the best you can hope for is a quick death.